I0553940

1939

Andrew Grogan

Published by Andrew Grogan, 2023.

1939

First edition. February 3, 2023.

ISBN: 978-0991159253

Written by Andrew Grogan.

Table of Contents

.... 1

The Sergeant Major 5

The Zepplin 20

Churchill 30

Hitler...59

Franco wins Spain...76

Troops on the Move...92

King Zog...132

Before the Storm...147

War 175

England..203

The Tunnel 225

1939

The Chronicles of Rishaan Finch

By Andy Grogan

1

I grew up hearing stories about wartime England—not from history books, but from my parents. They were children during the Second World War, and their memories weren't just about sirens and shelters. They remembered the smell of damp coats in underground stations, the scratch of name tags on their collars during evacuations, the strange excitement of watching the world around them change in ways they didn't fully understand. They remembered fear, yes—but also adventure, and laughter, and resilience.

As a writer, those stories never left me. They sat quietly in the background of everything I wrote, shaping the way I thought about childhood, danger, and imagination. I often wondered what it would have felt like to be a child at that time—not just a bystander to history, but caught up in it, shaped by it, surviving it in ways both ordinary and extraordinary.

This book is my attempt to capture that feeling—not just the facts of the war, but the texture of growing up in it. It's a story inspired by the fragments passed down at the dinner table, by the quiet bravery of a generation, and by the belief that even in the most uncertain times, there's room for adventure, mischief, and hope.

Andy Grogan
New York

The Sergeant Major

England, January 1939
THIS IS THE BBC CALLING:
German Foreign Minister Joachim von Ribbentrop visited Paris recently, where French Foreign Minister Georges Bonnet allegedly informed him, that France now recognizes all Eastern Europe as being in Germany's exclusive sphere of influence.
Bonnet denies making the remark.

Rishaan Finch knew he would never forget the war years; he had lost many people close to him. The storm of events that had swept across the globe in those turbulent years had changed him. He had learned skills that no normal boy should ever need to use and been in adventures that could fill several lifetimes of any other man. He had been a part of History and had seen History made around him. His story involved, among other things, an Indian Princess, a secret torn photograph, Nazi spies and a phantom Zeppelin. However, it first began with a strange telephone call that cold January day in 1939.

The day had already started oddly. He had heard on the radio that the Thames River had frozen over, and he wanted to see that for himself. First, he had promised his grandfather - the sergeant major - to recharge his radio battery at the local garage. His grandfather never left the house, due to his 'war wounds', and his home had not yet been wired for electricity. His grandfather would give him sixpence, but Rishaan was always happy to visit the sergeant major.

The roads were slippery and soot from the chimneys covered the London snow in a grey hue. The sky was overcast and the colour of lead. As he turned the corner of the road, he was almost bowled over by a huge man carrying coal to the houses. The man was covered in coal dust and growled at Rishaan to get out of his way. Rishaan found him fascinating. It was cold, yet the man was sweating from his labour. The sweat made white rivers down his black coal-dusted face that made it look like he was wearing war paint. The man returned from the neighbour's house after tipping the coal into the coal shed and returned to his horse and cart to get another load.

'Please sir, can I take your photograph? It's my hobby,' said Rishaan. He had decided that he wanted to be a photographer and a friend of his mother, a famous photographer, had told him the only way to get a good photograph was to be fearless.

'What's it worth to me?' growled the coal man. He had the same heavy London accent as his grandfather.

'I've got sixpence,' said Rishaan, pulling out the coin his grandfather had given him.

The coal man smiled, his white teeth set against his blackened face.

'Okay then, give me the money,' he said, seemingly intrigued by this posh, well-dressed teenager with an expensive camera and sixpence to spare.

Rishaan snapped some pictures as the coal man threw a sack of coal onto his back, then growled at Rishaan, making faces. They both laughed, and Rishaan thanked him. He knew the photographs would be great; he was looking forward to developing them.

'Thank you, sir,' said Rishaan, and the coal man nodded.

As Rishaan left, the coal man mumbled under his breath, 'Bloody rich kid,' but then put the sixpence into his leather waistcoat pocket. He would be having a pint at the pub on his way home.

Rishaan turned and watched the man leave. His horse followed him slavishly down the street, without any prompting from the coal man. Rishaan wondered what it must be like to be a coal man - to work so hard, in this cold, with little pay. He wanted to ask the man many questions, but he knew that he was lucky just to get the photograph. His was a different life from that of the coal man.

Rishaan's mother was an English journalist and photographer. His father was an American specializing in European affairs who worked as adviser to the American ambassador to London. They said he was President Roosevelt's eyes and ears in Europe, but Rishaan's father was always dismissive about this.

Rishaan had spent his early years in Washington, D.C., Berlin, Africa, Madrid and Paris. He loved traveling with his father and mother around the world. When he was ten years old, they moved to England for a quieter life, but Rishaan knew there were other reasons.

Rishaan loved London the most. His mother had told him so many stories about knights and castles and damsels in distress. He shared her love of history. Now he lived near Buckingham Palace, and he could visit the castles in England, including his favourite, the Tower of London.

Best of all, he could visit his mother's father, the sergeant major, whenever he liked. The sergeant major would tell him stories about his life in the army, his travels with Lawrence of

Arabia, the Great War, and his escapades with the Air Force in the Sudan and the Boer war. The sergeant major had served in several wars and had scars from every campaign to prove it. He looked like a sergeant major, with a large walrus moustache, waxed at the tips. He was a thin, sinewy man, with big hands (missing a few fingers) and a large scar running down one side of his face. He knew everything there was to know about horses, guns, poisonous snakes, Africa, Queen Victoria (whom he had met), and ancient Egypt. He had the tendency to tell long stories about the past and he would drift off into the worlds he had seen, sometimes staring into the distance, a sentence unfinished. However, when he told stories of the battles he had been in, he would bark his sentences like drill commands and his eyes would bulge as if he was blowing a bugle.

Rishaan was a bit afraid of the sergeant major's house. It was old and large, and had many rooms, even though the sergeant major only lived in the front room. The house had many smells, from a range of Oriental spices to strange smells of gunpowder and rotting military equipment. The sergeant major still lived in the 19th century; he sat at home at the window, wearing his pith helmet, and saluted strangers as they walked past his house. The sergeant major would keep watch on the area for attacking tribesmen, figments of his imagination. He slept in a tent pitched in the middle of the living room floor. Rishaan loved the old tent. It was dirty from many years of use and even had a few bullet holes in it. Rishaan's father said that the sergeant major had 'lost his marbles', but Rishaan thought the sergeant major was just doing what he liked best, and that was living in his memories. The old man found it comforting. He had lost so many friends.

'Tell me what you saw on your way here,' the sergeant major questioned him as he arrived.

'I saw two lions and a herd of wildebeest! I also saw a coal man who looked like he was wearing war paint,' offered Rishaan.

'Any Zulu tribes – did you hear any drums?'

'Not a soul. It's quiet in Notting Hill today; only the vultures and the apes were making any noise.'

This comforted the sergeant major. 'Then you may make me a cup of tea,' he commanded.

'Yes sir!' Rishaan saluted and went to the pitched tent in the middle of the living room and started the Bunsen burner to boil some water.

'Boil the water good; we don't want to catch any nasty tropical diseases. Then make the char strong son, it could be our last.'

Rishaan liked the sergeant major's moustache – marbled with nicotine stains, it did make him look like a walrus when it was not waxed. Rishaan wanted to have a moustache like that when he was older; he wondered how much he would have to smoke to achieve the same effect.

'When I was in Cuba I smoked cigars,' said the sergeant major, 'in Belgium I smoked shag, in the Middle East I smoked hookah. You could tell which continent I was on by the colour of my moustache.'

He had been awarded many medals, and he wore them with pride. Rishaan had never seen him without them, and maybe he would not have recognized him without them. It was the sergeant major's wish to be buried with his medals, his rifle, and a bottle of whiskey. In his coffin should also be a candle, a pair of scissors, a mirror, and a picture of the Queen. It was his fear that, after burial, he would come back to life again. The whiskey was to give him solace. The scissors, candle and mirror were so that he could keep his moustache respectable for the Queen.

His favourite story was about the sergeant major's socks. According to the sergeant major, his socks smelt of cheese.

'The cotton one's smell of cheddar; the woollen ones smell of Wensleydale. My old army socks smell of Gorgonzola, except the ones I had in the trenches: they smell of Brie, but that's probably because we were in France. I once won a contest where I could sort my socks simply by the smell. Now if that were an Olympic sport!'

'Yes, I know your father thinks I'm as mad as a hatter, and I know that there are no marauding Zulus in London; it just comforts me to keep a lookout. If you were there, at the Battle of Isandlwana, you would understand. I was about your age then.' The sergeant major never talked about Isandlwana. Rishaan always knew it was better not to ask. Maybe one day, when the sergeant was ready.

'Dad didn't say you were as mad as a hatter, he just said you had lost some of your marbles.'

'Only you could get away with saying that, Rishaan,' the sergeant major laughed. 'Anyway, when you've been chased around the world by the enemy as much as I've been, you're bound to lose some things along the way.'

The old man picked up a battered blunderbuss and started to clean it. Rishaan knew that whenever grandfather cleaned his gun the memories would flood back, so he sat cross-legged on the floor and waited patiently for his grandfather to tell another story.

'Every man is born with a certain amount of luck – some more than others,' he began. 'I was born with an incredible amount of luck – but every drop of my luck has been spilt on the battlefields of our Empire. One step outside the sanctuary of this house must now surely be my last.'

An old and moth-eaten lion's head was mounted above the mantelpiece, and in the head lived a mouse. This greatly amused the sergeant major, who would every now and then put some peanut butter on the lion's nose. 'Mice don't care much for cheese; it's peanut butter for them.'

As the sergeant major refused to leave the house, and Rishaan's mother refused to enter the house because of the mouse in the lion's head, they had reached an impasse in the family relationship. Rishaan was more than willing to act as an envoy, passing greetings and good wishes and biscuits made by the cook's help on a regular basis.

The sergeant major's house was filled with souvenirs from his different campaigns throughout Africa, the Middle East and India. He had Zulu spears and shields, medals and photographs, guns and bayonets and even a bomb with 'From Queen Vic' painted on it. There was an old canoe, African masks and headdresses, elephant tusks and a gun rack with different types of rifles, from an old elephant gun to a very dangerous looking grenade launcher.

He showed Rishaan the gun. It had a bullet hole through the breech. Every gun in the rack had been used in one campaign or another and showed the scars.

The things the sergeant major treasured the most were in the large front room; the rest of the house became more littered and untidy the farther away it was from the front. Mostly they were unused rooms, containing boxes full of stuff the sergeant major had collected. Rishaan was fascinated by the boxes but was also a little bit scared of looking inside. The sergeant major collected lizards and spiders, and he even claimed he had the left foot of a fallen comrade from a battle during the Great War.

'The Germans had dug a tunnel under our trenches, right under the spot where we were stationed,' he explained. 'It had been quiet – maybe too quiet, so I went off to get some more ammunition and check on the outposts. There was a God almighty explosion – it ripped the clothes off my body – I stood there butt-naked except for my moustache! My whole squad was wiped out. The only thing I found was Corporal Whittaker's left foot, in a helmet. I knew it was his – he was wearing his mountain boots; his Army trench boots had long rotted away.

I remember coming to France with Corporal Whittaker on the boat. As he watched the white cliffs of Dover fading into the distance, he said he had a funny feeling he would never set foot in England again. I told him that was nonsense, and I don't like being wrong. I promised his left foot I would bury it in England, and if and when I find it again, I shall most certainly do so!'

He even had shrunken human heads, kept in a box, which Rishaan still dared not open, which he had traded from some cannibals in the Congo. Written on the box, in doubtful red ink, was 'Heads – (shrunken).'

Rishaan knew that his father was involved in clandestine operations that he was not allowed to talk about. President Roosevelt was concerned about keeping America neutral since the American people were wary of another foreign war. He ached to tell the sergeant major about his father's work, but he knew to keep a secret meant to tell no one. Even his own father did not know that he knew.

'The British Empire was never the same after Queen Victoria died. But I blame the South African Boers, to tell you the truth. White men had not fought white men for more than fifty years, and we were convinced we were civilized. Well, that war proved us wrong, and the Great War proved us to be the barbarians we are,' he complained.

'If President Roosevelt would do a bit of sabre rattling now, then Hitler would back down. It's the same again and again; you should nip these things in the bud. Let it grow, and it'll take ten times the work to set it right again.'

Rishaan told the sergeant major of his plan to walk on the frozen Thames, but the sergeant major disapproved.

'I have some snowshoes upstairs somewhere – traded them for some scalps from a French man. He called them raquette à neige, snow rackets. Never had any use for them.'

Rishaan did not like the idea of going upstairs, but it was also intriguing to think what might be up there. The house was dark, even though outside it was a bright and clear winter's day, the snow reflecting light everywhere. The windows of the house were always shuttered, and the curtains were kept drawn. According to the sergeant major it kept the enemy outside, and they could not see inside. What light did penetrate the drawn curtains gave a cold blue tint to grey walls. The stairs creaked as if not used to carrying any weight for a long time.

The sergeant major had said that the snowshoes would be just laying around somewhere, not in a box, so that was good. Rishaan did not want to start looking in boxes. The rooms looked pale, with no carpets and wallpaper. Parts of the ceiling were starting to crumble and fall, leaving cracks that looked ominously like spy holes. In one of the rooms was an old lamp with 'Wehrmacht' written on it. He lit the wick, and a dull orange flame slowly glowed up, adding little light and plenty of flickering shadows. He checked the three bedrooms, among the spears and shields and German gas masks, but could find nothing. In one room, the African masks had been hung on the wall, and they all stared down disapprovingly on Rishaan as he searched for the snowshoes. There was that musty smell throughout the whole house, mixed with the occasional smell of some exotic herb, aromatic wood or some organic material decaying into dust that got more intense the deeper Rishaan went into the house.

There were several helmets – two French Adrian helmet's, three British Brodie helmets, worn by British and American troops, and a German Stahlhelm. Rishaan liked the Stahlhelm, and put it on, first checking to see if there was anybody's left foot still inside. He was not sure if all the sergeant major's stories were true, but it was not for lack of any evidence. The house was an unruly military history museum of the British empire of the last fifty years.

One box caught his eye. It had dark red stains on the outside that looked like bloody fingerprints. The box was too small to hold the snowshoes, but the intense curiosity that

Rishaan felt compelled him to look in the box. He walked over slowly. The lid was half open and he could see something inside – it looked dark coloured and there seemed to be several of them. There were some dark strands like hair, but he could not see if that was something else or was part of the other objects. He wanted to leave, to run, not to look, but his legs kept walking over to the box. He put his hand on the lid, and he slowly started to open.

Suddenly, Rishaan was startled by the sound of a ringing telephone.

It was a faraway sound, but not downstairs, where the sergeant major was. The sergeant major did not have a telephone as far as he knew; not many people did in those days. It was upstairs – in the attic. It was a muffled sound, but it kept ringing. Rishaan went over and looked at the small rickety ladder that led to the trap door in the ceiling. The ringing was coming from up there. He called down to the sergeant major but the sergeant major could not hear him – he had been partially deaf since a grenade attack during the Somme offensive. The attic was a strange place to have a telephone. He climbed the ladder. He had never been in the attic before—that was something he would never have dared—but again, his powerful curiosity compelled him. The trap door above his head was heavy, and it took all his strength to push it open just a little. It had not been opened in a long time. There was dirt in the cracks, and a cloud of dust fell onto him as he tried to push it open. He could just see inside. The attic was completely empty – strange considering the chaos in the rest of the house. However, in the middle of the attic, there was a small table, and on the table was a large black Bakelite telephone. It kept ringing. The bell sounded rusty and unused, but it was ringing.

And then it stopped.

Rishaan was disappointed; he would have liked to know who was on the other side. Why was someone phoning the sergeant major? Did the sergeant major even know he had a telephone? Maybe somebody had been calling the sergeant major ever since he had moved here, but being deaf, he had never heard it. It was a pity. Now he would never know.

Suddenly, the phone started to ring again. This time it seemed twice as loud. It gave Rishaan such a shock he nearly fell off the ladder. However, this time he was determined not to miss the call, and he pushed with all his might to try and open the trap door. It finally slammed open, and he rushed over to the telephone.

'Hello,' he said, his heart beating in his chest with excitement.

'Lionheart?' said a woman's voice on the other side. The line was very bad.

'Yes, this is the...' said Rishaan, but before he could explain who he was, the caller continued.

'... He wants to meet you – at the usual place. Friday at 09.00.' The phone clicked dead.

Rishaan wondered what that was all about, and as he went downstairs, he wondered if he would have to tell his grandfather. Would he be angry that he had gone up to the attic?

'Grandfather, did you know that there's a telephone in the attic?'

'Oh, er, yes, er, never use the bugger – did you find the raquette à neige?'

'It rang and I answered it.'

'What did she say?'

'How do you know it was a she?'

'Just tell me, what did she say?'

'A secret for a secret—why do you have a telephone in the attic?'

Rishaan's grandfather sighed. 'When I was a young soldier in the British Army, I got friendly with an officer. We would go off on adventures and we saved each other's lives a few times. Anyway, he returned to London and got involved with politics. He was very successful as well, sometimes high up in the cabinet, making decisions about war. However, as always in politics, sometimes you are out, and my friend would then find it very difficult to get information, information that would help him get back into an office of power. Information like how well the army was doing abroad. Information that was useful to him but potentially dangerous if it got in the wrong hands.

'So, we made a pact. I would supply him with information, if he would protect me and help me get the right postings in the army. To help me get information to him, he eventually had a secret telephone with a direct line installed in the attic. He would ask me to find out information and get me a posting were the action was. That's why I was in the Middle East a lot. Your grandmother used to give and take messages when I was away.'

The sergeant major sighed again, as if blaming himself.

'After that I returned to London. I never left the house after that. I never heard the phone ring again, forgot all about it. What did the woman say?'

'She said, 'He wants to meet you – at the usual place. Friday at 09.00.''

His grandfather went silent and stared out of the window. It was unusual for him to say nothing. Rishaan knew that this was serious.

'What does it mean?' he asked, but the sergeant major kept quiet. Rishaan knew it was useless to keep asking. The sergeant major was now far away, in the past, in some foreign land. After what seemed like a long time, the sergeant major looked at Rishaan. He seemed surprised to see Rishaan, as he had forgotten Rishaan was there. He stroked his moustache thoughtfully.

'You will have to go,' the sergeant major concluded. He did not seem to like asking Rishaan to do this, but he had thought about it and there was no other option.

'Go where?' asked Rishaan.

'To Egypt, my boy-Alexandria and to Cleopatra's needle! But it will be our secret; don't tell your parents. Just go there and meet the man, explain to him that an old war wound has kept me from coming but that you are trustworthy as a messenger. Tell him—tell him that if he hadn't had a Mauser at Omdurman, he wouldn't be standing there now.'

'What does that mean?'

'Let him explain.'

'But how can I get to Egypt by Friday, and without my parents finding out?'

'Ha – that's easy – just let Egypt come to you!'

Rishaan was confused but exhilarated. He felt a rush of excitement about this secret adventure, and if he knew the sergeant major at all, it was something very precarious and secret.

'What do I have to do?' he asked. The sergeant major explained to Rishaan that on the banks of the Thames there stood Cleopatra's needle, an ancient obelisk, imported from Egypt.

'Just get the message. The art of being a good spy is to listen, not to talk. And the man you will be meeting is a good talker. In fact, you might have trouble trying to get him to stop.' With this, the sergeant major laughed at his own joke.

'You said a secret for a secret. What is your secret, Rishaan?' said the sergeant major.

'My father is taking me on a work trip tomorrow. Something to do with an invention the British want to show to the Americans. I'll let you know more when I see you again.'

'Excellent,' said the sergeant major.

The Zepplin

The next day, Rishaan went on the trip with his father. He had been waiting for this day for a long time. This winter of 1939 was one of the coldest in living memory: snow covered the whole of Europe and rivers froze. However, Rishaan did not mind - he loved extreme weather. He was excited; he did not often get to see his father at work. Rishaan knew he worked for the American Embassy as 'a diplomat' but he was secretive about what it was he did. He knew his father was from a rich family, so he did not really have to work. His father was a quiet man but seemed troubled lately about the problems that were mounting in Europe. Rishaan suspected that his father was a secret agent, even though he could never get his father to admit it. Rishaan wondered about telling his father about the meeting he would be having on Friday but decided against it. His grandfather had sworn him to secrecy, but even so, his loyalties were to his parents.

Rishaan was proud that his father was American, and his mother was English. Sometimes he felt that he did not belong anywhere, that he was missing something other children had—a homeland. He thought he missed some sort of roots to a location, to a tribe. Despite this, this feeling of being different, he also felt he had something special.

Rishaan had discovered a secret about his father. His father communicated through his pipe. His father had the inclination to examine and clean his pipe whenever he was unhappy about something. If his father scratched behind his ear with the stem of his pipe, then he was thinking of a plan to make something work, like tuning the radio to get a German station. If he scratched his forehead then he was thinking of a good reason not to do something, like going to a fancy-dress ball. If he scratched the bridge of his nose, then he was about to tell a joke. If he rattled the stem of his pipe between his teeth, then he was about to suggest something that was a lot of fun, like going on a trip abroad. His father could never understand why he always lost at poker.

Rishaan's father never lit his pipe whenever Rishaan was around, as Rishaan had been very sick when he was a child in Africa. However, the pipe was always perched in his father's hand whenever he was not actively smoking it. Today he just chewed on his unlit pipe and, from the warmth of the first-class carriage, watched the people on the platform bustle around.

Rishaan wondered why his father was taking him along on the trip. He supposed that his mother had made his father take him on the excursion. She was always complaining that he did not do enough with his son. Rishaan did not mind. He was thrilled about the trip and glad that he had such an important father.

'They say that if there is a war you will not be allowed smoke a pipe,' said Rishaan.

'Now why is that, Kit?' said his father. His father always called him Kit, except when he was in trouble, and then it was back to being Rishaan.

'Well, they say that the Germans will send over planes at night that will drop bombs and the spies on the ground will gather near important buildings and smoke pipes so that the pilots will see them in a blackout.'

'You mean the spies will stand in the form of an arrow pointing at something that needs to be bombed, and then sneakily smoke pipes?'

'That's what I heard or at least something like that,' said Rishaan, not sure if his father was making fun.

'Well, then I shall have to do my utmost to stop a war in Europe!' said Rishaan's father.

'You could smoke your pipe upside down,' suggested Rishaan. Rishaan's father looked at him curiously and then pulled out his pouch of tobacco. He pressed the tobacco down tightly in the bowl, lit it, then turned the pipe upside down and smoked. The tobacco stayed in the pipe.

'Ingenious,' he contemplated. 'Strange though, it tastes slightly different, upside-down smoke. Problem solved, let the wars begin!'

Rishaan laughed, but started coughing at the smoke, so his father quickly extinguished his pipe. Rishaan hated it that his father could not smoke when he was there. Maybe that was why he did not see much of him. Rishaan thought that his father looked angry because he had to put out his pipe. His father was indeed angry, but angry with himself. When Rishaan was sick, with a tropical disease called cholera, his father had sat next to his bed and smoked his pipe to keep the mosquitoes away, but the smoke had only made Rishaan worse. Although his parents had never talked about it, he had nearly died from the disease.

Rishaan felt a little jolt as the train began to move. The steam plume from the engine almost filled the whole station and covered the carriages. As the train gathered more speed and pulled away from its own cloud of steam, Rishaan watched the disappearing city as they slowly travelled to the outskirts of pre-war London. Little did he know that many of the buildings he saw steaming by would be damaged or destroyed in the next few years.

Rishaan could see the children playing in the streets, many in ragged clothes. There was a market where people bought cheap vegetables and a flimsy merry-go-round where children stood by, hoping they might get a free ride. There was an old woman, sheltered from the cold by several layers of rags. She was dragging a broken bag weighed down with wood and was having great difficulty with her burden. Nobody stopped to help her. She quickly disappeared into the distance as the train forged onward to the countryside. Rishaan took a photograph of the industrial London landscape.

As the train gathered speed, the city changed into countryside and the grey buildings gradually disappeared. Instead, snow-covered hills started to surge and roll past. Their blinding whiteness reminded Rishaan of the hills and dunes in the Sudan. He remembered being on a train with his father on their way to Khartoum. A group of local bandits had chased the train. His father thought they were Mahdists, a Muslim group, but he was not sure. When they started shooting at the train Rishaan's father looked concerned, but Rishaan thought it was great fun. The bandits had no chance of catching the train and their bullets seemed ineffectual. It was something special when his father pulled out a revolver from his attaché bag. He did not know his father even had a gun, let alone carried one with him.

'Do you remember those bandits in the Sudan?' he asked his father, and his father laughed.

'It's not as warm here as it was there,' he said.

Rishaan tried to fantasize about the bandits shooting at the train, charging through the snow on their beautiful horses. Then, almost as if the train engineer could feel their presence, the train started to pick up speed.

Rishaan loved Africa; it made him sad to think the reason they left was because he had been sick. He knew his parents loved it there. Rishaan remembered little of that time. He did remember in the six months he took to recover; he learned to speak Arabic with his Sudanese nurse. The sickness had left him with streaks of grey that was visible against his jet-black hair. His mother said it made him look very distinguished, and it certainly made people look twice at him.

It also left him with a dark secret that frightened him. The doctors had told his parents that the disease might have affected his heart. He did occasionally feel dizzy, but he never let it get in the way of his sports, especially cricket. However, he lived with the possibility that he might become ill again at any minute. His parents kept it a secret from him, but a servant had accidentally let the secret out; she had not understood that he was not supposed to know. Now Rishaan knew and in turn he kept that a secret from his parents. He did not want them to worry; they were too protective of him as it was.

Rishaan's condition had its uses; he had noticed that adults were kind and tolerant with him. They answered his questions with much more patience than they showed any other children. It was fun being special.

Once, when his great-grandfather was on his deathbed, he had asked to see Rishaan alone, which surprised everyone in his large family. The room was dark and there was a musty smell to it. The old man lay there. His face was the oldest Rishaan had ever seen, and he made a gasping noise at every breath.

'Rishaan,' he said, his throat parched and soft, almost a whisper. 'This is just between you and me. They told me when you were sick in Africa that the doctors said you died once, and it was a miracle that they could bring you back to life.' He leaned closer to Rishaan, as if to ask him a secret. 'What was it like - to die?'

Rishaan did not really know how to answer. He could not remember much about it. He was often delirious with fever. He slept badly; his nights filled with nightmares. His great-grandfather looked at him. His eyes were full of fear, his hand trembled as it clasped Rishaan's arm. He had never seen his great-grandfather afraid; he had been such a strong man. Rishaan thought about it for a while. Then he leaned over and in a whisper, he said, 'Great-grandfather, I can only say that dying is easy; it's the trying to stay alive that's difficult.'

The old man stared at Rishaan for a few seconds, then the fear left his eyes, and he smiled. 'I guess you're right,' he said.

As he watched the people in the English countryside pass by, Rishaan wondered what it would feel like to be poor. He felt privileged, but at the same time guilty. He did not like feeling guilty; it was not his fault that he was 'fortunate'. That was the word, 'fortunate', that his father used when he talked to him about it. He knew that his parents' wealth would make sure that he would never want for anything. He felt like ignoring it; it was just the way things were. He even thought about blaming the poor for their predicament, but he knew that that was too easy. It was not so much the differences in the rich and the poor that disturbed him, but the reality that there were a great deal more poor people than rich. Many more. His father had told him that it was his good fortune to be from a privileged family, and it was therefore his duty to make the most of it, to seek out and learn from the experiences that his destiny had chosen for him.

'Always ask, always learn, always try to understand,' his father had said. 'Try to be the best person you possibly can. But never forget, we're fortunate, a very fortunate family.'

Rishaan thought about this as the train raced south. He remembered something someone had said about the rich.

'Father,' he asked, 'are we old fortunate or new fortunate?'

Rishaan's father frowned. 'Upside-down pipes and old and new fortunate—child, you spend too much time with your mother.' Rishaan smiled.

There had been a lot of discussion the last couple of months about whether Britain should go to war with Germany. Rishaan's mother was for appeasement, trying to keep Hitler in check with diplomatic talks and sanctions. Rishaan's father was for war, but this was a family secret. As an American and as a diplomat, he was supposed to keep a neutral position. Rishaan was undecided. The whole country was tired of war. The Great War was just twenty years ago, and it seemed like everybody in the country had lost someone on the battlefields. One of the things that Rishaan remembered when he came to live in London was the extraordinary number of men missing an arm or a leg that he saw on the streets.

The name of the German 'Reichskanzler' Adolf Hitler was always in the newspapers, always on the radio. The adults talked of nothing else. Nearly everybody was for appeasement. There was a British politician who was calling for war with

Hitler, but he was considered a warmonger. Rishaan's mother said that if that man kept calling for war, she would make sure he would not be invited to Chelmsford House again, but Rishaan knew she did not mean it. She was too much of a journalist to do that.

Rishaan took more pictures from the train. He loved photography; for him it was a way of capturing memories. Sometimes he took pictures of the countryside, other times of people on the platforms of the stations. Some people looked very poor and lost. Rishaan wondered if they were the German and Polish refuges his mother was talking about. These were the people escaping persecution in their home countries. They looked cold and frightened.

Soon the train pulled to a halt. They were in at the most southern part of England, near the White Cliffs of Dover. A car met them at the station and took them to the government research facility, close to the edge of the cliffs. It was a strange and bleak looking building, with sentry guards stamping their feet in the cold, trying to keep warm.

The scientist they met at Dover looked exactly like an eccentric English professor. He was thick set, with a bald head with long strands of dark hair combed over his large dome of a scalp. He had thick round glasses that magnified his pupils. He wore a large white scientist's coat that was a little too small, and his stomach threatened to pop the buttons. He had a bumbling manner and spoke fast, often the next sentence being started before he could finish the first.

The scientist looked disapprovingly at Rishaan but then almost immediately forgot about him as he launched into a monologue about his research. 'So good to see you, Mr. Finch,' he began. 'We are very excited about what we are doing here and I'm sure you Americans would love to see what we have cooking.'

The man showed them around the building. It had a large antenna, many noisy machines, which the scientist called 'terminals', and a round television screen that reflected perfectly in his round glasses as he talked. The scientist gave Rishaan some paper and pencils to draw with, then started to explain the secret workings of the machines he called Radar to his father. He talked about making a breakthrough using the radio lower frequencies, which he thought the Germans knew nothing about.

This bemused Rishaan; it seemed odd to him that some adults thought making a 12-year-old draw a picture rendered him deaf. They had hardly begun to talk when the scientist got very excited.

'Look at that! As if they knew you were coming!' he said, pointing at a small white mark on the screen.

Rishaan and his father were not impressed.

'What is it?' asked Rishaan's father.

'I'll show you,' said the scientist, and he led them outside to a path that ran down to the edge of the white cliffs. All they could make out was cloud and sea.

'Watch over there,' said the scientist, pointing toward a cloud. At first, they could see nothing, but slowly a part of the cloud darkened. At the same time, this darkened area cast a shadow on the sea below.

'It's a Zeppelin!' shouted Rishaan.

'Well done,' said the scientist. 'The Germans have been sending Zeppelin Airships over; I think they are probing our radar stations. They don't know what they are, and they are testing us.'

Rishaan's father was impressed. 'So, you could see the Zeppelin with your machine before you could see it with your eyes?' his father asked.

'These Airships are hundreds of feet long and only travel at a top speed of 70 miles an hour, so you'd think our fighters would spot them and shoot them down easily. However, in the 20 raids they made on London during the Great War, not even one was shot down. The fighters could not find them in time. They would fly in high above the clouds. Sometimes they would hide in the clouds, and the fighter planes could not fly in after them without fear of a collision. Now we can see them coming from over a hundred miles away, and we know where they are. With my machine, London is safe!' he declared.

Rishaan always had his Leica camera with him, and he took some photographs of the Zeppelin. It looked amazing as it floated slowly, approaching the coastline. It was like a huge, majestic animal, like a whale, as it turned and started following the coast, incapable of broaching land. The Zeppelin could not pass over sovereign territory without permission; England and Germany were not at war.

'These are for the sergeant major,' said Rishaan, taking more photographs.

Churchill

Back in London, the day after their trip to Dover, Rishaan's father was listening to a repeat of the New Year's Concert of the Vienna Philharmonic Orchestra on the radio. Johann Strauss II's 'Blue Danube' filled their large London home in Westminster. Rishaan loved listening to the radio with his father, especially the news and sports. Rishaan was especially proud when his father tuned into the distant German radio stations and asked Rishaan to translate. Rishaan had found it difficult at first, listening and translating at the same time. Nevertheless, it was like anything difficult: the more he practiced the better he got. Rishaan's school holiday would end on the Monday the 9th of January, in the new year 1939 - but till then he was free to do what he wanted. He was going to join a new school, Balminster, and was excited to meet new friends. He had been to many schools, so joining a new one was not challenging to him anymore. The trick was to walk in with confidence and treat everyone as if you were old friends.

Rishaan said that the music on the radio was not to his taste, but he really needed an excuse to go that secret meeting he had. Also, he still wanted to walk on the frozen Thames. He wanted to walk along the river and see London from a unique view, walk up to the houses of Parliament, and walk under the London Bridge and the Tower Bridge. He was not going to tell his mother—she would never let him walk out on the ice—so he said he was going to visit the sergeant major, which he would do on the way. Then he would not be lying.

He got dressed in as many layers of clothes as he could and made his way to the river Thames. It was freezing outside; London was white with snow, and a misty fog drifted up the Thames giving it a mystical quality. Rishaan had never been anywhere so cold. At the river embankment was Cleopatra's needle, an obelisk from Alexandria in Egypt. The sergeant major was right; Egypt had come to him. It stood proudly at almost 67 feet tall; the top was difficult to see in the mist. The Thames had frozen over and Rishaan could not see the other side through the cold haze. Luckily, there was no wind; otherwise, he would not have been able to stay long.

Behind the monument, some steps led down to the river. Although Rishaan was on time, the man had not yet arrived, and after a while, Rishaan began to think it was all a hoax, one of the sergeant major's jokes. Rishaan went down the steps and stood on the ice. The ice creaked and groaned. It did not seem strong enough to hold his weight, and Rishaan could not see anybody else out on the ice. It was still early though, and very cold. Maybe there would be some people later, when the sun had come up and warmed the air a little. Rishaan did not think it wise to go out on the ice alone, just in case he got into trouble.

Gradually, as if materializing out of the mist, a portly man with a bowler hat and a cigar appeared at the top of the steps. At first, Rishaan could only see a silhouette; the morning sun backlit his form, and the cigar smoke made it look as if he was breathing fire. He looked old, as old as the sergeant major, he used a cane to support himself, and he seemed familiar. Rishaan knew that he had better introduce himself, as the man was probably expecting the sergeant major.

'How do you do, sir,' said Rishaan. The man looked down at Rishaan but did not seem to be very interested. Rishaan recognized him: it was a friend of his father's, Winston Churchill. He had been to dinner a few times, and Rishaan had seen him at the American embassy. Rishaan's father said that he was the only Englishman to see the peril of Hitler. He was the politician who was trying to get Britain to declare war on Hitler, the one Rishaan's mother called a warmonger.

'My father says you're the best politician in England.'

'I know I am, now bugger off.'

Nevertheless, Rishaan was not to be daunted. He ran back up the steps toward Mr. Churchill and stuck his hand out. 'My grandfather sent me. Lionheart. You're waiting for him. He said he can't come because of an old war wound. He sent me as a messenger.'

Churchill looked at the boy. He recognized the same features as the sergeant major and remembered the boy from his visits to his father's house. The curious grey streaks of hair. He remembered the story about Rishaan's illness in Africa. So, he decided to take a friendlier tone. He shook the boy's hand with a strong, decisive shake.

'Did you know that this is a real obelisk?' he asked, pointing at Cleopatra's Needle with his cane. 'It's from around 1500 BC, originally made by Thutmose III but then used by Cleopatra to honour Mark Antony at a temple at Alexandria. They are amazing pieces of stone. They were later toppled and buried in sand, which helped preserve the inscriptions from weathering. Six men drowned trying to get it to London; the barge it was on broke free in a storm in the Bay of Biscay.'

'Look at the sphinx's paw,' he continued. 'Do you see the holes? They were caused by shrapnel from when the Germans bombed London during the Great War. They used Zeppelins then, now they've got fast flying aircraft. There are three Cleopatra's Needles. One is in Paris and another in New York. I predict that if we don't do something soon about Hitler, they will all be in German territory before long.'

Rishaan had seen the damage to the paw; there were many holes in the thick metal. Anyone standing nearby would not have had a chance.

'I saw a Zeppelin at Dover. I took some photographs,' said Rishaan.

Churchill patted Rishaan on the head and smiled, then taking a puff on his cigar, he walked toward his chauffeured car that was parked close by. It was clear the conversation was over. 'Send my regards to your grandfather, and your parents,' he called, dismissing Rishaan.

Rishaan was disappointed. He felt intimidated by the old politician, but he did not want to let this go so easily. Rishaan wanted to give the sergeant major a secret message, but bringing Churchill's regards was not what he was expecting.

'If you didn't have a Mauser at Omdurman, you wouldn't be here now,' called Rishaan. He did not really know what it meant but it was his only chance.

Churchill paused, puffed his cigar, then stepped into the back of his car and closed the door. It is getting cold, thought Rishaan. His hands and feet were freezing but he stayed where he was. The car remained standing, but Rishaan soon became so cold he decided he had better go back to the shelter of the London Underground. As he walked away, Churchill wound down his window, a cloud of cigar smoke erupting from the cabin like a volcano.

'Get in,' he said. He sounded as if he already regretted it.

Rishaan ran to the car and got inside. Rishaan liked the Rolls Royce Wraith Limousine, and it was nice and warm. Churchill had some blankets, and he made sure Rishaan was wrapped up.

'Where does your grandfather live now?'

'Westbourne Park Road.'

'Well, let's take the mountain to Mohammed. Driver! Westbourne Park Road!' called Churchill, and they set off.

They stopped at the traffic lights at the Houses of Parliament. Rishaan remembered something his mother had told him. 'Did you know that these traffic lights were the very first in the entire world? They were gas lanterns then, with semaphore arms, but they kept burning down.' Rishaan loved London; it was full of History. Churchill smiled.

'What does it mean, that if you 'didn't have a Mauser at Omdurman you wouldn't be here now'?' asked Rishaan.

'Well,' said Churchill, 'it's Lionheart's way of telling me that I must be patient. When I was young, I was in the Army, and I went to India. We went by troop ship, and it took us nearly a month to get to Bombay. When we finally arrived, I was as impatient as anything to get off and explore the marvels of India. However, there were formalities, and we would have to wait in the harbour for several hours more. I, with my usual brashness, managed to get permission to leave earlier, on the condition that I arranged my own boat. This I did, there being a shoal of tiny skiffs all around. We paid some rupees to a ferryman, and he took us to the dock. However, in my haste when trying to get to the slippery stone steps, I grabbed an iron ring. Just then, the boat swung away, and I wrenched my shoulder. I managed to scramble up onto the dock, but my right shoulder had been damaged, and now I must be most careful, or I can dislocate it at a sneeze.

'I later I had the honour of taking part in the last cavalry charge of the British Empire in our attempt to capture the Sudan from the Dervishes at Omdurman. I was all fired up and ready to go, but your grandfather convinced me to take a Mauser pistol instead of a sword – my gammy arm would never have had the strength to hold a sword up, let alone kill a man with one.'

Churchill looked out of the window at the wintry London. 'What a contrast this is to that hot, hot desert of the Sudan. Ask your grandfather to tell you about the Dervishes, the warriors of the Sudan. The bravest men that ever walked the earth.'

'I know,' said Rishaan. 'We lived in Khartoum for a while.'

Soon they arrived at Westbourne Park Road, and his grandfather was very pleased to see Churchill. 'You're looking very good, sir,' he said, and saluted.

'You're looking pretty good yourself, Lionheart,' said Churchill. Churchill didn't salute. 'You never salute when you are in civilian clothes,' he whispered to Rishaan.

'Let us not fool each other; we have become two old men,' said Churchill.

'Tea for the gentleman,' ordered the sergeant major, and Rishaan began to brew up. Churchill looked at the tent pitched in the middle of the room and at all the souvenirs. He walked around the room, looking at the spears and shields and guns.

He was quiet for a while, just like the sergeant major could be. He too seemed transported back to another time, another world.

'Khartoum?' asked Churchill quietly, as if he already knew the answer, pointing at a shield with his cane.

The sergeant major nodded.

'Aqaba?' asked Churchill again, holding up a keffiyeh, the traditional Arab headdress.

Again, the sergeant major nodded. 'That shemagh belonged to Lawrence of Arabia.'

'Bangalore?' asked Churchill, this time tapping a polo stick with his cane.

'Hyderabad, 9-3 against the Golcondas—do you remember?'

'Could I ever forget? That polo stick might even be mine...'

Churchill picked up an army water bottle, from a box containing about ten.

'I'm always prepared for the wilderness, sir; there are too many dangers out there for us not to be prepared,' the sergeant major informed Churchill. The sergeant major had wondered how well Churchill would remember him, but he could see that for Churchill the memories were flooding back.

'And we have experienced a great many dangers together, sergeant major, but I would happily have them all again instead of the political wilderness I'm in now.'

'I've always agreed with you, sir, what you said about Hitler. It's just the British people are tired of war. They thought the war to end all wars had ended all wars. I know Chamberlain is trying to stop war, but that's what's he supposed to do as

Prime Minister. But if Hitler makes any more trouble, I'm sure you'll get back into Parliament, as sure as India is British.'

'I hope not, but if so, then I hope so.'

Rishaan brought the tea, and Churchill sat in the chair across from the sergeant major, who scanned the horizon for bandits and marauders. Rishaan sat cross-legged on the floor.

'Your grandfather was a very creative soldier, my boy. We were once sending an expedition up the Mamund Valley in India. We were having trouble with the local bandits and Sir Bindon Blood, our commander, had ordered us up the valley to teach the Mamunds a lesson. Tactically, this was not a good thing to do, especially as the valley was blocked with mountains on three sides. At the end of the valley we got into a fight with some of the bandits and we were pinned down. We had to send a message back to get some reinforcements, but which of the messenger boys was the most reliable?

'We also had a problem in that we thought that one of the boys, a local, was in fact betraying us. Your grandfather had a brilliant plan. He told the local messenger boy to go back to the base camp and ask for reinforcements, and to give an accurate location of where we were pinned down. He then wrote the same message, asking for reinforcements and giving the place, on a hardboiled egg. He did this with a mixture of alum and vinegar. The solution penetrates the porous shell and leaves the message on the egg white. This is only readable when the shell is removed. He also wrote that if the messenger boy's message was the same as on the egg, then he was to be trusted, and if not, off with his head! The reinforcements came, and I never saw the messenger boy again!'

'The good old days!' The sergeant major laughed. 'But of course we should never forget Mr. Churchill's unique recipe for invisible ink.'

'Urine is cheap, effective, personalized and in moments of intense danger, readily available!'

Rishaan was fascinated. These old gentlemen had lived a great life; he wished that he too could have such an interesting existence.

'And it is from your talents in the science of secret codes that I now seek advice, sergeant major,' said Churchill, pulling out a piece of paper from his jacket.

'I have a connection in Germany. He is a very brave man who has been close to the Nazi rearmament program. After the Great War, the Germans were only allowed to have 100,000 men in their army, and no airplanes. This piece of a paper is part of a message sent to me by this man with proof that the Luftwaffe, the German air force, not only exists, but is more than six times the size of our own air force!'

'What is it we can do to help?' asked the sergeant major.

'The information was sent in code. My man in Berlin said he would first send the documents in code, and then he would send the solution to the code by a different route, just in case the wrong people found the documents. I have these papers, but he didn't have time to send me the information on how to crack the code; he was arrested on charges of espionage. They have no evidence whatsoever, so he might go free, but I dare not try and contact him because that might raise suspicions. The only message I got was that you, sergeant major, were the key.'

'Me?'

'Yes. I've tried to get some of my contacts at military intelligence to crack the code, but my name is becoming more and more unpopular at the War Office. I have a reputation as a warmonger, a bloodthirsty troublemaker. There have been a few red herrings as well. Their codebreakers have been told not to look at my informant's papers, and I'll be damned if I can make heads or tails of it.'

'Show me the paper,' asked the sergeant major.

It was just the first few sentences from the original document, and it was total gibberish.

GAL ALPQNCUT GAL DA 209 V1 NSFG SF 1. SUTUPQ 1938 PQSQQ WHEAJ PJRM ZAJTQA GSPP GJA DSPRMJFA PAML PRMWAL ZU NCJATAN WSL

'Why would he mention me? Do I know him?'

'No, but he knows you. We were talking about how to code his messages before he went back to Berlin. I mentioned your egg trick. He said it would take enough eggs to feed an army to get all the information across.'

'Can I look please?' asked Rishaan

'No, sorry boy, these are government secrets, and you have not taken any oaths of allegiance or vows of secrecy.'

'I promise not to tell,' assured Rishaan, rather optimistically, 'and anyway, if it's in code I won't be able to understand it!'

'This boy, Mr. Churchill, is the most inquisitive, energetic, probing, curious and opportunistic boy one would ever have the misfortune to meet.'

'I have little reason to doubt you, sergeant major.'

'He speaks several languages, having travelled the world and attended several international schools and having the privilege of many indigenous nannies.'

'My Arabic is not very good; everybody knows I'm English when I speak Arabic.'

'Do they!' said Churchill, amused. 'You are a young Lawrence of Arabia!'

The sergeant major was still studying the paper. 'When your connection in Germany mentioned that I was the key, could he have meant this?' asked the sergeant major, who then rolled up his sleeve to show a large key-shaped scar on his forearm.

'I had forgotten about that,' said Churchill, who then rolled up his shirtsleeve to reveal a smaller round scar.

Rishaan looked confused. 'What's that?' he asked.

'After the encounter Mr. Churchill and I had in the Sudan, we were almost immediately shipped out back to England. Mr. Churchill was sent back because the cavalry was too expensive for Lord Kitchener's needs. I was sent back because I had inflicted a nasty wound to my arm. A dervish spear! Mr. Churchill was keeping me company on the ship back home. The wound was becoming more infected and refused to heal. I was becoming more delirious as the fever and infection grew. There was a risk of gangrene, in which case my arm would have to be amputated. The doctor said there was only one solution, and that was to skin the wound. This involved taking a piece of healthy skin the size of a large coin, with a little bit of flesh attached, and grafting that over the wound. The doctor looked around for a volunteer, and Mr. Churchill was chosen.'

'It was very painful,' added Churchill. 'The doctor took a razor and flayed a piece of skin from my arm. It took all my nerve not to pass out, and a stiff brandy to stop my hands from shaking. But the sergeant major didn't lose his arm, and I have a scar as a souvenir.'

Rishaan grimaced, and the two old men laughed.

'Could this be what he means by the key?' asked the sergeant major.

'I don't know. I didn't tell my contact in Germany about that—at least I don't remember.'

There was a knock at the door. It was Churchill's chauffeur. 'It's time to go, sir,' the chauffeur said, 'if we're to make the meeting at the Admiralty.'

'Yes, I'm coming. Anyway, sergeant major – does this mean anything to you?'

The sergeant major shook his head. 'May I keep the paper?' asked the sergeant major. 'Maybe I can remember something.'

'Of course,' said Churchill, and with a tip of his hat, he was gone.

'A Great man, Winston,' said the sergeant major, as Churchill's car drove down the road. 'I hope the Zulus don't get him on the way to the Admiralty.'

As he watched him go, the sergeant major remembered something from the Great War. 'We were fighting in the trenches. They had called in some clever lads to figure out where the Germans where and what they were doing. They had learned a trick from the French. They listened to the German radio operator's sound as he rattled off the Morse code. Dot Dot, Dash Dash, Dot Dash. They had found that each operator had a unique 'fist' – a speed and a way of signalling that, with a lot of practice, they could recognize. Like a handwriting. They also tracked the radio waves to locate the source of the radio messages. They knew which signature was with which battalion, so by listening to the messages they could tell where each battalion was, even though they could not decipher the code. If the battalion moved over a few days, they could make a guess which direction they were going in, and what they were going to do. Sending a message, even though it can never be read, is a dangerous thing to do.'

'It's time to exchange some secrets,' said Rishaan. He had a deal with the sergeant major: if Rishaan had a secret to tell he would tell the sergeant major, who rewarded him with one of his own secrets.

'Look at these pictures,' said Rishaan. He pulled out the photographs he had made in Dover. He had developed them himself in his homemade darkroom. He showed the sergeant major the photos of the coal man, which looked amazing, and then the photos he had taken at the White Cliffs of Dover.

'Ah, yes – the dreaded Zeppelin,' said the sergeant major, perching his reading glasses on the end of his nose to study the aircraft more. 'I remember during the Great War, I was in London on leave, when there was a raid. Terrible machines of mass destruction. But this is no secret, Rishaan,' he said.

'There's more. I was with father and a scientist showed us a machine that can spot them hundreds of miles away. He said that was enough warning for our fighter planes to shoot them down.'

Rishaan pulled out the drawing he had made at the Radar station. It was a sketch of the monitors and the terminals. He had noted that they used low frequency radio waves, to remind himself to find out what that meant later. The sergeant major was impressed.

'Now tell me one of your secrets. It had better be good; my secret is excellent.'

Rishaan's grandfather stroked his moustache. 'Let me think. Ah, yes, I know of a secret tunnel in London. A tunnel that goes to the very heart of government. Even the officials at Whitehall don't know where it is.

'Really! Where is it, where does it go?' asked Rishaan.

'Now that's another secret, isn't it?' said the sergeant major.

'That's not fair!' protested Rishaan.

Rishaan's grandfather laughed. 'I guess not. I won't tell you where it starts, but I'll tell you where it ends. It goes all the way to 10 Downing Street. I once used it when I had to deliver some secret documents to Ramsay MacDonald about the Levant.'

'You will tell me some day, where the tunnel starts?' begged Rishaan.

'When and if the time is right' said the sergeant major. He knew he had to be careful with Rishaan.

Rishaan earned another sixpence by taking the sergeant major's other radio to the garage to have the battery recharged. The sergeant major always had two radios; he never wanted to miss anything. As Rishaan waited, he thought about the message and the importance of cracking the code, so Churchill could have proof that Germany was rearming, and therefore planning to expand into Europe. He wanted to crack the code, but to do that he needed a sample of the message, so he needed to convince the sergeant major to give it to him. It would be difficult; the sergeant major was a stickler for following orders.

When the battery was charged, Rishaan went back to the sergeant major's house. The sergeant major was sitting at the window with his blunderbuss across his knee, but he had fallen asleep, his Pith helmet pulled down over his eyes, and only his red nose and large moustache sticking out. What luck! The piece of paper was in his top pocket, and the temptation for Rishaan was just too great. Rishaan carefully crossed the creaking wooden floor and reached over to pluck the paper out of his pocket. The blunderbuss pointed straight at Rishaan's stomach. If the sergeant major were to startle awake and fire the gun, Rishaan would have no chance.

He pulled the paper gently out of the pocket; the sergeant major did not stir. The lines of code made no sense at all, but that was nothing but a challenge to Rishaan. He quietly left the room and searched through a few boxes to find some paper to copy the code. He found something that looked like a map that was blank on the back. He diligently copied the code, checking to make sure he had done it right. If he had made a mistake, he would later be trying to crack a code that was wrong, and that would be a waste of time. After checking it three times, he quietly went back to the sergeant major and replaced the paper. Little did he know, as he left the room, that the sergeant major smiled a little from underneath his pith helmet.

As he walked down the road through the snow, Rishaan looked at the code again. It meant nothing. There were a few numbers, but were they in code as well, or part of the key? There was a fog, mixed with the smoke of a hundred thousand chimneys, that covered London in a blanket and made Rishaan cough. He needed to pay attention to where he was, or he could get lost. Rishaan had to go home first; he had his housework to do, and then it would be getting late. He hated doing his housework. It was at his mother's insistence, but Rishaan thought it was something the servants should do, and they were paid for it, anyway. His mother said that he should always understand that any mess he would make was his responsibility. When he mentioned that the servants tidied up after her, she said that was different. He was old and wise enough to not to push that argument.

When Rishaan arrived home, his parents were getting ready to go to a party at the prime minister's office at 10 Downing Street. They were in the main living room in their house in Rutland Gate. Rishaan watched them. They had not seen him, and he thought them a happy, loving couple together. The room was lit by the fireplace and some candles, giving its Edwardian interior a warm orange glow, casting shadows on the silk curtains. His mother looked beautiful in her long black gala dress with the mother of pearl necklace that she had been given by her grandmother. His father looked handsome in his tuxedo. They were an attractive couple. His wife helped him with his bow tie.

'I hope it won't be a serious political discussion tonight. It's been nothing but Hitler, Hitler, Hitler ever since the Kristallnacht,' said his mother.

'Thousands of Jewish businesses destroyed in Germany, nearly three hundred synagogues burned, thousands of Jews arrested—what is the point of it? The British are also confused about America's attitude toward Hitler, especially since Time magazine made him Man of the Year. We should be building a new world after the Great War, the War to end all wars, not this pettiness,' Richard sighed. Rishaan could see that his father was spending a lot of his time on this issue. He looked worried.

'Well, I think he's a very obnoxious little man. I did not like him when we met him in Berlin; he has that look in his eye. Disingenuous—that is the word I was looking for, disingenuous. Even though I'm taller than he is he still managed to look down on me. I do hope that the Prime Minister Neville Chamberlain is up to him.'

'He didn't like me at all, but he was probably just envious of my beautiful wife,' said Richard, trying to make light of the conversation. He wanted his wife to enjoy the evening.

'Yes, now that you mention it, that was probably it,' she laughed.

Richard smiled. 'Hitler asked me how I had become a special envoy to the ambassador, so I told him about my study at Harvard, my work in the army, my service in the public sector... Then he asked me about my father. He even asked if he was Jewish! When I said he was William Finch, the industrialist, he guffawed! He guffawed! Reason enough for a war right there. He probably thought that I had bought my success with Daddy's money. He liked Rishaan though, but who doesn't? He thought it very amusing that an American boy could speak German. He taught Rishaan how to say a few words with an Austrian accent.'

Julia became serious. 'Well, tonight I hope you will be more social. Talk to people who are not at the top of the power tree. You should get more involved with small talk.'

'Darling, I don't do small talk, I only do big talk,' joked Richard.

Julia gave him a disapproving look. 'Well, I need some contacts if I'm going to get any work done, darling. See if you can get any of your cabinet minister friends to help me,' she warned him.

'Politicians are wary of the media darling, especially a woman reporter with a reputation like yours.' Richard knew that British politicians were not as media hungry as the Americans. Also, he had the suspicion that his wife was planning something—some new story to report, some cause to get involved in. She always had something up her sleeve.

'I just want to write about the people, the citizens who get mixed up in the wars,' she pleaded. 'Just like the Spanish civil war. They think it is all about charges of infantry and how army officers distinguished themselves. We need to know more about the civilians and the refugees—the effect on the civilian population.' Richard could already see she was passionate about it.

'Well, I'm glad you're not jumping onto tanks in Spain anymore—not in your condition,' Richard retorted. He was getting more protective of her. There was too much of the sergeant major in her adventurous spirit.

'There you are, champion!' said Rishaan's father, suddenly spotting him in the doorway.

'Where have you been?' said Julia.

'I was at grandfather's. And I met Mr. Churchill – it was spiffing; they showed me their scars!'

'Don't you dare mention Churchill tonight,' said his mother to his father. 'That will set them all off and that will be the end of the evening.'

His father laughed. 'Agreed, we will send Hitler and Churchill to Coventry tonight.

What was Churchill doing at the sergeant major's?' asked Rishaan's father.

Rishaan was taken aback by the question and cursed himself for giving so much away. He decided to change the subject. 'Can I come to the dinner with you tonight?' Rishaan asked.

'I'm afraid not, Rishaan, I have the suspicion that it's going to be a very work-oriented evening,' replied his father, giving his wife an apprehensive look. 'What was Churchill doing at the sergeant major's?' asked Rishaan's father again. He was not fooled by Rishaan's manoeuvring.

'They are old war friends and Churchill had dropped by to reminisce,' said Rishaan, thinking on his feet. He never wanted to lie to his parents, and he had not, but for some reason he felt he had to be discreet with the truth.

'The cook has prepared a meal for you,' said his mother, saving him from further explanation. 'The governess will make sure you get to bed on time. Don't give her a hard time, Rishaan, I know she's different from the other nannies; you can be a demanding and over-resourceful young man when you want to be. Yes, very tiring indeed.' Then she kissed him on the forehead.

Rishaan's mother left to get ready for the evening, so Rishaan took the opportunity to ask his father about secret codes. Although his father would never admit it to Rishaan, he sometimes worked with MI-8, the American Secret Service, sometimes called the Black Chamber. The Americans had never really developed an effective secret service by 1939, mostly because they were so far away from any real potential enemies. Little did Rishaan know, his father was the most advanced spying system they had. 'Gentlemen do not read each other's mail' was the maxim of the American State department.

'Father, how would you go about breaking a code?'

Rishaan's father looked bemused, 'What are you up to now, you rascal?' His father was getting suspicious.

'Nothing, I was just wondering. I saw some coded text at grandfather's house, and it looked so devilishly complicated. I would not know where to begin to try and break it.'

'Well, I don't know much about the techniques they use to break a code, but it is decidedly difficult. The secret to a code is to try and get the key. The key is always the weakest link in a code. If the person you don't want to read the message gets hold of the key, you might as well write the message in plain English and save everybody the trouble.'

'But if they don't have the key, is it still possible to break the code?'

'Well... sometimes. Someone once told me how they did it. It's done by analysing the frequency of the letters. If you have the coded text, then you try and find patterns. For example, the letter E is much more frequent in the English language than, for, the letter Q. So, if in your coded text there are a lot of, for example U's, then this might be the letter E. In addition, the word 'The' and the word 'and' are very common. So, if you see clusters of three letter words you could try substituting the letters for these common words. With these kinds of tricks, it possible to make guesses about words, and then you can start filling in the blanks. It's like a crossword puzzle. If you have guessed right, then words will start to appear. Guess wrong, and you must start over again.'

'That reminds me of Mary, Queen of Scots,' said Rishaan's mother as she returned, looking beautiful in her black dress and pearls, her blond hair just touching her milk white shoulders.

'You look ravishing tonight, darling,' Rishaan's father said, and Rishaan noticed that goofy look he got on his face whenever his mother dressed up for a dinner party.

'Thank you, dear,' acknowledged his mother, as if she had just thrown something on and it was nothing special. Adults were funny sometimes, thought Rishaan

'Tell me about Mary, Queen of Scots,' said Rishaan, trying to bring his parents back to earth.

'She was the cousin of Elizabeth I, the Queen of England. Mary wanted to be the Queen of England, and as a Catholic had the backing of the Catholics. Elizabeth was supported by the Protestants. There was a great deal of religious tension in the British Isles in those days. Anyway, Mary had fled to England after unsuccessfully trying to take the throne in Scotland. She was arrested and placed under house arrest.

'There was a plot by Anthony Babington to kill Elizabeth and put Mary on the throne, but if the plot was to be successful Babington needed Mary's blessing. As she was under house arrest, he could not ask her directly so he used a courier. A Catholic priest called Gifford was asked to smuggle her messages, which he hid in the hollow bung of a beer keg. Unfortunately, Gifford was a double agent, working for Elizabeth's principal secretary, Sir Francis Walsingham. So, every time Gifford was sent to smuggle a letter to Mary, he would first make a detour and take the letter to Walsingham's code breaker. Walsingham wanted proof that Mary was plotting against Elizabeth, so then the Queen would have no other choice but to behead her cousin.'

'Babington wrote to Mary telling her about the scheme, so Walsingham was already warned and had Babington followed. However, he wanted Mary to write back giving her consent and therefore implicating herself in the plot. She was scared that if Elizabeth was murdered, she might be murdered the same day in revenge, so she insisted that she would be freed from the prison just before the assassination was committed.'

'So, Walsingham had the proof to charge Babington and Mary with treason, but Walsingham was a shrewd spymaster. He wanted the names of all the conspirators. He added some text to the end of a letter Mary was sending back to Babington asking about the other members of the plot. Babington dutifully wrote back, still thinking that the code was safe, telling Mary about all the other plotters. Walsingham then arrested all of them, tortured them, and not surprisingly, they all confessed. Elizabeth had no choice but to have her cousin tried for treason and beheaded.

'Babington and his conspirators tried to escape, but after 10 days they were caught and brought to London, where they were hung, but before they were dead, they were taken down, their guts were taken out and then they were cut into four pieces.'

'What a terrible thing to do to someone,' said Rishaan

'Yes, it was a punishment only meant for the crime of treason. When Elizabeth heard how much the men had suffered, she ordered that the rest of the conspirators, who were to be executed the next day, should only be hanged.'

'Well yes, that's enough blood and gore for one evening,' said Rishaan's father.

'They were not all cruel in those days,' said Rishaan's mother. 'Women who committed treason were simply burned at the stake.'

Seeing his mother silhouetted against the flames of the fire, talking about being burned at the stake, made Rishaan uneasy. 'Don't ever go committing treason, Mother, promise me,' he said, and hugged her.

'I promise, especially tonight, as guests of the Prime Minister.'

'Well, we had better start making a move; otherwise, I will be hung, drawn and quartered by the ambassador,' said Rishaan's father.

'But how did Walsingham crack the code?' Rishaan asked his mother.

'I am sorry, Rishaan, I do not know, but maybe we can ask at the party. It wouldn't surprise me if there were a few experts in subterfuge there tonight.'

'It will be an ice breaker, at least,' replied Rishaan's father.

'Let's walk through Green Park. It's good to get some exercise before we must sit in that smoky room at Downing Street.'

'Good idea, darling. I'll tell the chauffeur, but I'll tell him to pick us up at the end of the evening. It's cold now but there might be a blizzard tonight. We don't want to be found frozen to death in the centre of London, do we?'

'We're a jolly bunch tonight. Anyway, it will never be as cold as that time in Moscow. You know how I hate the cold,' she laughed.

'Don't remind me. I have not yet decided if I have forgiven you or not.'

'Forgive me,' she said, kissing him on the check.

'You're forgiven,' he laughed.

Rishaan's father pulled the thick mink coat tight around his wife and then they walked into the dark wintry night. They laughed at the cold and the foolhardiness of walking to 10 Downing Street. Rishaan waved from the dining room window. It was warm with the fire raging, but Rishaan could feel the chilly air through the glass.

As they walked down the street, they hugged each other. 'Don't get too cold now darling,' he said. 'I can always call a cab.'

'Don't fuss, sweet, you know I don't like it when people fuss. There's enough suffering in humanity without me getting any attention. There are a great many people in this world who would gladly swap their circumstances for me with my rich husband and warm expensive mink coat.'

'Yes, but you're pregnant and you are such a handful at times. I know where Rishaan gets his energy from that's for sure...'

'Do you think Rishaan suspects? Do you think he knows that he will have a brother or sister in seven months' time?' Julia asked.

'Probably—he's much too smart for his own good, but it's best to wait another month or two before telling everybody you're pregnant, just to make sure you're in the safe zone. That's what the doctor said. Anyway, it's bad luck to tell everyone too early.'

Rishaan watched them disappear into the darkness, but his mind was already wandering elsewhere. He was confused. There were now several questions that were still unanswered. First, why did grandfather really have a telephone with a direct connection with Winston Churchill? This would be difficult to find out. The sergeant major was good at acting madder than he was when it suited him.

Second, he needed to find out more about Churchill. He had visited his father but so had many famous people. Who was he exactly? This he could ask his father, but he would have to be careful; his father was suspicious already.

Third, he had to crack the code. This would be the hardest part. After his parents had left, he went downstairs to the kitchen and sat at the large oak table. The cook and her two helpers were busy cleaning and cooking, and Rishaan liked the company. They gave him his dinner, which he ate in the kitchen. The governess, a tall bony woman with thin lips, came and checked to make sure Rishaan was not in trouble but soon left. Rishaan didn't know what to think about her. He had had no problems with her; she mostly left him alone. She had tried to teach him some French, but Rishaan spoke it fluently, and he sometimes even had to correct her awful accent. His mathematics was on a par with hers and his geography was much better, especially as he had been to a lot of countries already. Soon the governess was just giving him homework and leaving him to get on with it. They had an unspoken agreement: if he got his work done properly and on time, she would not bother him too much.

Rishaan pulled out the piece of paper he had copied at the sergeant major's house. It meant nothing to him. Even with his knowledge of languages, he could see nothing familiar in the words.

One of the cook's helpers, Esther, was new. After they were finished, she came over to talk to Rishaan. She was about twenty and pretty, with jet black hair and brown eyes. She had a sad look about her, as if she had been through a lot.

'The cook says you speak German,' she said in German.

'Tatsächlich,' replied Rishaan.

'It is so good to hear my mother tongue again,' she sighed. 'I do miss it so. My English is not so good, and my poor mother cannot speak it all. Yet we're so lucky to be here.'

'You are from Germany?' asked Rishaan.

'Yes, we're refugees, that is—my family. My mother and father and my sisters came over here from Germany, after the Kristallnacht – the night of the broken glass.'

'What happened? What does it mean, the night of the broken glass?' asked Rishaan. He had heard some things about it on the radio but wanted to know more.

The girl seemed frightened and looked around her, as if to look for German storm troopers in the shadows of the kitchen. 'The Germans were deporting the Polish Jews from Germany into Poland, 17,000 of them. They just threw them out of the country, but the Poles just sent them back. It was a nightmare; people were starving on the roads—old people, children. The Polish government finally put them into camps, but the conditions were terrible. A Polish Jew in Paris tried to petition the German embassy but was rejected. In frustration and anger he shot one of the embassy staff. Hitler was furious, and he ordered his thugs to smash up all the shops and businesses owned by Jews. That's why they call it the Kristallnacht – the night of the broken glass. The streets in Germany and Austria were littered with the broken glass of shop windows. Fifteen hundred synagogues were damaged or destroyed, along with many Jewish cemeteries and more than 7,000 Jewish shops and department stores. Some Jews were beaten to death while other Jews were forced to watch. Thirty thousand Jews were arrested and taken to camps, especially the young men. I was with my grandmother when it happened. They left my father—he was too old, I think—but they took my nephew. He escaped. We got a letter from him; he is in Norway. I hope he will be safe there.

'My grandmother had a shop in the centre of Munich. We heard the smashing of glass and the shouts of the thugs. We went upstairs and hid in the attic. My sister was terrified, which helped me take my mind of what was happening. I was too busy trying to keep her calm. Grandma wrapped us in a blanket and hid us behind some boxes.

'The thugs soon came to our shop. They ransacked the goods, smashed the windows. I think they were getting tired. My grandmother went downstairs; they just ignored her, although one brute did push her out of the way. My father said that Hitler's thugs still didn't have the total backing of the people, so they were careful not to offend too many citizens. But my father said that they would get bolder. Later, after they had gone, I went out into the street. It was littered with broken glass; the moonlight glistened on the broken shards. Some of the citizens were still on the streets. I thought they might have been sympathetic, but they were indifferent. It was as if they thought we Jews had brought it on ourselves. I knew then that my father was right; we would have to leave Germany. I didn't want to come to England. What if England declares war on Germany? What would that make me? A German enemy in England?

She switched to English. 'Thank you for listening to me. It is so good to be able to speak my native language occasionally.'

'I think your English is good, considering you have only been here a few months,' said Rishaan.

'Thank you. You should talk to Maria, the other maid. She's Spanish. Cook said you speak some Spanish as well. Cook likes you; she says you're so clever. Maria is also a refugee. Her parents were Spanish republicans during the civil war in Spain, and they were killed at Guernica. Your parents were very kind to give us work. Your parents are good people.'

Rishaan realized that his parents had taken on more staff than they needed, just to help these refugees. They were lucky, and he felt lucky to have his parents.

That night Rishaan lay in bed, thinking about the Kristallnacht. It must have been frightening for Esther; she had lost her motherland, lost her friends and had to flee to another country. Rishaan realized that his nomadic life had been one of choice, of free will. It must have been terrible to be forced to go.

Rishaan thought again about the code that he had copied from Churchill. He looked at the piece of paper, under the sheets of his bed, using a torch. He could make neither head nor tail of it. He fell asleep and had a vivid dream of being trapped in a burning house, the flames getting closer and closer.

He awoke still tangled up in the sheets, with his torch shining in his face.

At breakfast, feeling unrested from his fitful night, he looked at the code. Maybe there was a solution for this. Today was a new day, and he knew what he had to do. It was time to visit Brian Smith-Woberton.

Hitler

THIS IS THE BBC CALLING:

Today, Hitler gave a speech before the Reichstag calling for an 'export battle' to increase German foreign exchange holdings. He makes a 'prophecy' in which he warns that if 'Jewish financiers' start a war against Germany, the result will be the annihilation of the Jewish race in Europe..

Brian Smith-Woberton was a school friend of Rishaan's who had a great talent for taking everything mechanical or electronic apart and putting it back together again in a better and unique way. Fascinated by technology, he knew everything about radio, and could tinker for hours at the bits and pieces of apparatus, staring at his inventions through thick, round glasses. His father was a rich inventor with more than 200 patents, and he let Brian experiment with gadgets and electronics. He was the same age as Rishaan but was portlier built. He was bad at all sports except one, wrestling, in which he was undefeated. Rishaan went to Brian's house in Park Crescent, near Regents Park.

'Hello Brian,' said Rishaan, looking around in wonderment. Brian had his own hobby room, and it was filled with books, bits of what seemed like small steam engines, telescopes (most of which were in some stage of dismantlement) and all kinds of stuffed animals. Rishaan doubted if there was anything still in one piece. Every time Rishaan visited the room looked different, but always a mess.

'Rishaan! Great you are here – I'm working on my two-way radio; you can help me!'

There was a peculiar smell in Brian's room, a mix of soldering iron and singed carpet.

'Lend me a hand with the solder, Rishaan. I really loved that book you lent me, 'Halliburton's Book of Marvels'. I thought it just spiffing how he climbed Mount Fuji in the winter! And how he swam the Panama Canal—what a hoot he managed to swim through the locks by registering himself as a ship and paying 35 cents' toll!'

'I can lend you his 'Second book of Marvels' – he goes to China and meets the emperor, and he says that you can see the Great Wall of China from the Moon! But I guess we will never know for sure, will we?'

'It was a great story about him breaking into the Taj Mahal at night and swimming in the pools. I've heard he's got a new scheme planned: he's going to sail a Chinese junk from Hong Kong to San Francisco – I can't wait to read all about it in his next book!'

'I've got a real cracking story for you,' said Rishaan, and he showed Brian the coded message.

Rishaan told Brian all about the sergeant major and what his father had said about frequency analysis. Through it all, Brian just stared at the piece of paper. After Rishaan had finished Brian took off his glasses, cleaned the dirt off with the tail of his shirt and then looked again at the piece of paper, as if wiping away the grease would help crack the cipher.

'Spiffing!' said Brian and stared at Rishaan in disbelief. 'Absolutely spiffing!'

'Well, we need the key, that's for sure,' said Rishaan.

'Why can't we try frequency analysis?' asked Brain. Rishaan was impressed.

'Well, there's not enough text. There's not enough to see if there is any frequency. I only had time to copy this much, but there is more.'

'Well, we need it. Can you get hold of it?' asked Brian.

'I can try, but it will be difficult.'

'Then let's split this task into two. My brains and your derring-do,' said Brian. 'You try and get the rest of the text, so we can try frequency analysis, and in the meantime, I will try and see if I can figure out the key. Maybe I can build a machine that can do this automatically!'

Rishaan thought this was an excellent plan, but he wondered how he would be able to get the rest of the text. Churchill had all the documents. The rest of the day Rishaan helped Brian build his new two-way radio. It was primitive but it finally worked, and they had great fun sending messages to each other inside the large house, then trying it outside in Regents Park.

Rishaan thought about a plan that would help him get the rest of the coded document, but he was sure that if Churchill found out he would never give his permission. Maybe he could get the sergeant major to help, but if he asked, the sergeant major would probably say no and then he would be alert to what Rishaan was trying to do. There was only one thing for it, and Rishaan knew what he had to do.

It was a few days later before Rishaan had the chance to visit his grandfather again. It was still very cold, and the streets were slippery with ice. His parents were busy organizing some trip his mother was planning. He didn't know what it was, but it kept them distracted and out of his way, so he managed to slip out.

The sergeant major was pleased to see him, and to hear that the Zulus had gone back to Africa for the winter.

'My first army gun was a Peabody-Martini-Henry, but if you make me choose, it's the P14 Enfield for me. Saved my life three times, it did. That is my Webley Revolver—that's what I had when I took Jerusalem with General Allenby. That's where I got the nickname Lionheart.'

'Don't blame them,' he said, leaning his blunderbuss against the wall. 'I almost wish I could go with them... That's an old black powder elephant gun. I had it back bored to give it more velocity and make it lighter. The Americans call it 'wildcatted',' said the sergeant major, pointing to a large gun leaning against the wall. 'Hell of a kick—knock me off me horse, it did, when I first fired it. It still wasn't always powerful enough on the skull for a frontal brain shot on an elephant. You had to know what you were doing standing in front of a charging elephant with that thing in your hands. If your gun bearer didn't get the loaded guns to you quickly enough, or you couldn't keep on your horse, that was that. After that I got a .470 Nitro Express. We put extra nitro-glycerine in the gunpowder. That did the trick.

'We used them during the Great War. The Germans used to send their snipers out into no-man's land with a thick sheet of metal for protection. Our Enfield bullets would just bounce off them, so I got out my .470 Nitro and blew a hole the size of a football in it. They never bothered us again. I once saw a German use a black powder elephant gun against a tank. It didn't do much, but the smoke it gave his position away. Covered his face in black powder – looked like a Zulu, he did. I made sure he never bothered us again either.

'Is it all right with you if I go and look at some of your souvenirs?' asked Rishaan, as innocently as he could. 'They are very interesting.'

'Sure, see if you can find a left foot. I've looked everywhere but I can't find it'

'I'll do my best,' said Rishaan.

At first, he just looked around at the boxes on the first and second floors. He did not want the sergeant major to get suspicious. It was strange, but now that he was scared about what he was going to do, the boxes did not seem to bother him all that much.

When he thought that the coast was clear and that his grandfather was sleeping, he climbed the ladder to the attic and with all his might he pushed open the trap door. It slammed open, giving Rishaan a shock. He listened to hear if the sergeant major had heard, but there was no noise below. Rishaan thought that the sergeant major was probably still asleep. If there were Zulus in London, they would have absolutely no problem in taking sergeant major by surprise.

The room had not changed a bit. It was dark and dusty, still completely empty except for the small table and the black Bakelite telephone. Rishaan walked slowly toward the telephone, as if it was a highly sensitive bomb. He didn't know where he was getting the courage from, but he knew that it was something he had to do. Finally, he lifted the receiver up and put it to his ear. All he could hear was a constant droning noise. How stupid could he have been, he thought. He would need a telephone number to dial. He was just about to put the receiver down again when there was a change in pitch in the ringing sound, a clunk as if a connection had been made, then a woman, the same woman who had rung before, said 'Yes?'

'I have a message for Sir Winston Churchill,' said Rishaan, in the deepest voice he could manage.

'And that is?' asked the woman.

This threw Rishaan a little. He had not expected the woman to be so cooperative. He had expected her to ask difficult questions or even see through Rishaan's subterfuge.

'Tell Sir Winston that we may have cracked the code, but we—I mean I—need the rest of the document to analyse.'

'I shall give him the message,' said the woman, and she hung up. She was a very pragmatic lady.

Well, that wasn't too bad, thought Rishaan. But what was going to happen now? Would Churchill get the message, and if so, what would he do? What if Churchill comes round and gives the document to Grandfather personally, or phones Grandfather to inquire about his method of analysis? Rishaan began to think that he had not thought things through enough. Maybe he should let the sergeant major in on his secret.

When he went downstairs, the sergeant major was brewing some tea. 'Did you find it, the left foot?'

'Er, no, only a right foot, sorry...'

'Very funny, never mind – it couldn't have walked away on its own, ha!'

After tea Rishaan left, promising the sergeant major to keep an eye out for any strange animal tracks in the snow. Rishaan began to worry a little; maybe what he had done was – treasonable!

That night in bed, Rishaan reviewed what had happened. It was all ill-conceived and badly executed.

First, he did not know if anybody would answer the phone; if they did, who it would be; and if they would believe him when he lied. Maybe they would ask awkward questions, for which he would have no ready response. Had he been lucky? The lady on the phone had simply said she would give the message to Churchill. Even if she did give the message to Churchill, would he believe her, and would he simply send the coded documents to sergeant major? Rishaan began to regret the whole thing.

A few days later Rishaan went with his father to meet Hans Hooschspier, Rishaan's father's counterpart at the Dutch embassy. They had known each other in Washington, D.C., and they occasionally met to keep ahead of the unofficial news. Hans's son, Wouter, was a great friend of Rishaan's; they had often played together around the Lincoln memorial or visited the Smithsonian Institute.

They walked through Green Park. It was cold, but the air was crisp, and the sky was clear enough to warm the face. Then Rishaan and Wouter ran and chased each other, as their father's talked business. Rishaan was tempted to tell Wouter about his adventures with decoding the documents for Churchill, but he knew it was not wise to go into too much detail. He should not tell anybody, or at least only if it was very necessary. Still, it was such fun! Wouter would really appreciate it; it was such a great lark and a tremendous yarn! Rishaan decided to tell him the basics, leaving out that it was Churchill who had given him the code. Wouter loved the whole story and kept asking for more details and saying he wanted to help. Rishaan swore him to secrecy but promised to reveal more as things went on.

They ran through the park, kicking up the snow, running out onto the frozen pond and chasing the ducks and geese that were standing around. Wouter threw a snowball that hit Rishaan on the back of the head, making his cap fly off.

'Raak!' shouted Wouter. Rishaan knew in Dutch it meant 'a hit!"

'It seems Holland has just declared war on England,' shouted Rishaan. 'We had better inform the diplomats.' They looked at their parents. They were at a distance, engaged in a conversation, and looked preoccupied. Rishaan saw his father give Wouter's father a brown envelope; he looked sombre and troubled. Rishaan was intrigued; he knew that his father was greatly concerned with the developments of rearmament in Germany. Rishaan wondered what he would make of the documents he had translated for Churchill. Whenever Rishaan asked him about Germany and Hitler, his father always gave the government's position, which at this moment was neutrality. However, Rishaan had picked up enough signals to know that his father was against taking a neutral stand toward Hitler. Rishaan was convinced that his father had the assignment to help Europe try to contain the problem, but he had to do it in a covert way to maintain neutrality.

He then wondered if maybe his father might be interested to see the contents of the documents that Churchill had given him. He knew that Churchill knew that his father was an important man at the embassy. Maybe Churchill was manipulating him! Maybe Churchill was hoping he would show his father the documents! His gut feeling was that this was not the right thing to do. If Churchill had wanted his father to decrypt the message, he would have asked himself.

Rishaan did not have much time to ponder this, as he received another snowball that knocked his cap off again.

'Treffer!' shouted Wouter.

'Let's go to the Natural History Museum!' said Rishaan.

'Yes!' said Wouter. 'It will be like ours visits to the Smithsonian!'

They asked their parents, who were still preoccupied in their discussion, and they agreed and gave the boys some money for the underground and some sweets.

'Be back by 6 o'clock, Rishaan,' said his father to the boys, as they ran off toward Buckingham Palace.

Rishaan decided he had better not tell Wouter anything more about his adventures with the secret documents. If he told Wouter, he might tell his father, who in turn might confront Rishaan's own father with the secret. Rishaan still had to figure out the best thing to do.

They got off the underground at South Kensington and walked around the museum. Rishaan loved the large diplodocus dinosaur that greeted everybody at the entrance. Wouter loved the terracotta tiles, which were used mainly to protect the building from Victorian pollution, and the beautiful stonework depicting plants, animals and fossils.

The next few days Rishaan spent visiting the sergeant major, who was starting to get suspicious.

'I am very popular these days, Rishaan,' he said, in a voice that betrayed what he was really thinking.

'I just like coming around here,' said Rishaan feebly.

'You're not the only one. Winston Churchill was around this morning.'

Rishaan could feel his whole world collapse in on him. He was caught red-handed. Now Grandfather and Winston Churchill would be infuriated with him.

'He gave me the documents I asked for,' said the sergeant major.

'Sorry,' said Rishaan. He tried to look as remorseful as possible.

'It's a good job an old soldier like me can think on his feet. Winston was in a hurry, so he didn't have time to stay and ask awkward questions. He did say that this was the only copy, he didn't have the resources to get someone in a typing pool to make a copy.' The sergeant major gave him the document. 'It'll be our secret, Rishaan. Winston can't crack the code; if he could he wouldn't be asking me. And I can't crack it either; believe me, I've tried. If you want to have a go, well it's the best shot we have.'

'Thanks sergeant major. Gosh, this is exciting; you wouldn't believe how much I've been thinking about it. I'm going to get right on it.'

'It is exciting. It's always a great feeling to be challenged. Yet so many people do everything they can to avoid it. It is ironic that at the height of a battle, one feels so alive, yet that is the time one has the greatest risk of losing one's life!'

Rishaan could see that the sergeant major was starting to reminisce about some battle he had fought in, and normally that would have been fun, but Rishaan wanted to start work on the document, so he stuffed the documents into his satchel, made his excuses and left.

Rishaan took the underground back to Regents Park. He wanted to get to Brian's as quick as possible. It seemed like all of London was in the tube, bustling to get from one side of the city to the other. It was quite hot in the station, after the arctic cold outside. It seemed that everybody was reading a newspaper, and the main topic was the antics of Hitler. Everybody agreed that he was a madman, but the majority was for appeasement. On the train, Rishaan took a quick look at the secret document. There were pages and pages of incomprehensible code. The pages were covered with corrections. It was obvious that the typist was not very experienced and had made the documents in a hurry.

Rishaan changed at Oxford Circus. Normally he would have walked to Regents Park, but it was cold outside, and he wanted to study the document some more.

Some youths about Rishaan's age were running up and down the platform, causing trouble. They were over-excited, pushing and shoving each other. One of them had grabbed the satchel of a smaller boy and they started throwing it to each other. The little boy could only stand helplessly by and watch. Then suddenly, one boy lunged too far to grab the satchel and accidentally pushed a woman off the platform on to the tracks. She wasn't hurt, just shocked and angry, and told the boy what she thought of him. Just at that moment, there was the signature rush of air as the train came closer to the station. Rishaan hurried to help her, dropping his own satchel and putting out his hand to quickly pull her back on to the platform. The train driver saw her and slammed on the brakes, but he would never have been able to stop in time. All the passengers in the train fell forward at the sudden deceleration.

Together with two other men on the platform, Rishaan managed to pluck the woman back onto the platform, like pulling a fish out of a lake, just as the train screeched past.

'Are you all right?' Rishaan asked the woman. She promptly gave the boy who had accidentally pushed her a mighty wallop on the ear, which seemed to echo around the station. Everybody cheered.

'I am now,' she said.

Rishaan laughed, but he felt his heart pounding rapidly in his chest. He was relieved. It was a close call, he thought. Then another shock – his satchel was gone – the bag with the documents. He looked frantically around. At the far end of the platform, he could see some of the schoolboys running off, and one of them had his satchel.

'Stop!' shouted Rishaan, but they just started to run faster. Rishaan knew he would never be able to catch them, but he was certainly going to try.

Rishaan ran down to the end of the platform, by which time the boy with his bag had turned a corner and run off down one of the tunnels. Rishaan knew that he there was a choice of two tunnels he would have to make, and after that several more. The chances of him finding the boy and the bag were remote. The platform and tunnels were jam-packed with people; Rishaan had to weave in between the milling crowds.

He ran down one tunnel, could not see them, and then ran down another. This was a disaster! He had lost them among the other passengers. Had the boy gone to another station, or had he taken an escalator and left the underground altogether? After searching frantically, Rishaan had to concede that he had lost the trail. The boy and the satchel were gone. He had lost the documents. How was he going to tell the sergeant major? What would Churchill say? This was the only copy. Maybe this would have been the definitive proof Churchill had needed to show that Germany was treacherously rearming.

Rishaan was despondent. He walked back to the station platform. There was only one thing to do, go straight back to the sergeant major and tell him what had happened. There was no point in putting it off. It had happened, and he would find out in the end, anyway.

'Is this your bag, me old China?' asked a schoolboy. It was no ordinary boy. He was huge, built like a circus muscleman. His school uniform hardly fit him, and his school cap looked tiny perched on the top of his head. He held Rishaan's bag out, the strap held between two fingers as if it weighed nothing. Rishaan was overjoyed.

'Oh, thank the Lord! Yes! Thank you! Thank you!' It was only then that Rishaan saw that the giant had a boy's head trapped under his left arm. He let out a faint squeak.

'What do you want me to do with him?'

'I think you've already done it,' said Rishaan.

The giant lifted his arm, and the boy fell to the ground.

'You brute – you nearly suffocated me!' he gasped.

'It's still alive,' said the giant, surprised, at which the boy let out another squeak and quickly scurried off.

'You don't know how happy I am to get this bag back,' said Rishaan.

'Strange,' said the giant, 'most lads would be pleased with the excuse for not giving in their homework.'

'This is not homework,' said Rishaan.

'I know,' said the giant. 'I saw you running after the boy, who doubled back on you. That's when I clobbered him. But you had run off, and I didn't know if I would be able to find you. Lucky for you that you started to walk back as well. Anyway, I took a butcher's hook inside to see if I could find some sort of identification. Very interesting!'

'Er, yes, well, er, it's a project for school.'

'Is it?' asked the giant.

'My name is Rishaan.' He stuck out his hand.

'My name's Rupert, but my friends call me Sam, short for Samson.' He shook Rishaan's hand with a grip that made Rishaan wince.

'It looks like a coded message,' said Sam, bringing the subject back to the document.

'Er, yes, well, er, it's a school project,' said Rishaan again, but he knew it was a feeble excuse.

Sam said nothing, but just looked at Rishaan, expecting more. Rishaan noticed that Sam was still holding onto the bag.

'Really?' said Sam.

'Well, not really, but I'm not allowed to tell anyone. I promised my grandfather.'

'Are you going to tell your grandfather that you lost the secret coded documents on the Oxo?'

'Oxo?'

'Oxo cube - tube, underground.'

'Well, not exactly, no. I think that that kind of information is on a need-to-know basis. And he doesn't need to know.'

'So, I guess Mr. Winston Churchill definitely doesn't need to know either?' said Sam.

Rishaan groaned. Churchill's name was on the envelope, and a note with Churchill's name on it was inside.

'Let me in on the secret,' said Sam. To show he was to be trusted, he let go of the bag.

Rishaan clasped the bag to his chest. He was so glad to get it back.

'OK,' said Rishaan. 'I'm on my way to a friend of mine. He is helping me crack the code. If you come with me, I'll fill you in on the way.'

'First-rate!' said Sam, and with a hard slap on Rishaan's back, they went off to visit Brian.

Rishaan clutched the bag tightly on the subway to Regents Park, and he told Sam the basics of why he had the documents. Then a thought struck him. 'Wait a minute; did my grandfather pay you to keep an eye on me?'

'No. He paid me sixpence to keep an eye on the documents.'

Rishaan had to laugh; he should have known. 'He's not so crazy after all,' said Rishaan.

'He told me to make sure that the Zulus don't get hold of them.'

'He's as mad as a fish,' agreed Rishaan.

'Yes, but I'm saving up for a Raleigh bike with the Sturmey Archer three-speed gear hub, so I don't mind looking for Zulus in London at sixpence a go.'

'There's another thing,' said Rishaan. 'It's a great coincidence that, the first time ever for me, my bag gets stolen.'

'Yes,' said Sam, 'I had thought of that. I think those boys might have planned to apple bob your bag. They first created a diversion, and when you were distracted, they took their chance.'

'Why would they want the documents, or rather, how would they even know about the documents?' asked Rishaan.

'They probably don't. They most likely don't know what they are. Which makes it worse—they were most likely paid to steal your bag by somebody else. That complicates things. Somebody is after the documents.'

'Who – the Germans?' said Rishaan and immediately regretted it.

Sam looked quizzically at Rishaan. 'Germans?'

Oops, thought Rishaan, I should not have said that. 'Well, yes, it might be German documents, but I'm not sure.'

'Ok, so we might now be followed by German agents, who are trying to get their hands onto these secret coded documents that come from Winston Churchill, the famous Nazi hater,' concluded Sam.

'Well, I guess,' said Rishaan. He was obviously not good at keeping secrets. He would have to work on that.

'Which means that security might have been compromised?'

'Again, correct,' confirmed Rishaan.

'Bring on the Zulus,' sighed Sam.

Back on the underground, they both looked around the train carriage; the passengers looked at the same time very innocent and deeply suspicious. Nobody looked like a German agent, but Rishaan wondered, what does a German agent look like? There was the man in the leather jacket, sitting at the far end. He was with his girlfriend, but maybe they were both agents – a clever disguise.

'Follow my lead,' said Sam. The train doors were just about to close at the next station when Sam pulled Rishaan up out of his seat, and they jumped out of the carriage. They stayed on the platform, Sam looking to see who had disembarked with them, and if they had done so also at the last second. The station was built on a curve, so it was difficult to see if there was anyone who had gotten off at the front or back. Also, a lot of people had gotten off at this station, so it was hard to keep track of all the faces.

'Follow me,' said Sam, and they raced into the tunnels connecting the three tube stations that connected at Oxford circus. After backtracking, they took the train to Regents Park, then Rishaan took the initiative, leading Sam into the park where they dodged around, then climbed over the back garden wall into Brian's Garden. Tom the gardener was busy clearing away some snow.

'What are you doing, master Richard?' asked the gardener.

'Just avoiding some German agents—hope you don't mind, Tom,' said Rishaan.

'Fair enough,' said Tom and he continued his work.

Franco wins Spain

THIS IS THE BBC CALLING:

The Spanish Civil War has officially ended as the last of the Republican forces surrender. Dictator Francisco Franco has assumed power in Madrid.

The American adventurer Richard Halliburton delivered a message to his fans from a Chinese junk, before leaving on a voyage across the Pacific Ocean.

Neville Chamberlain has just given a speech in the House of Commons offering the British 'guarantee' of the independence of Poland.

'I know I should support you in everything that you do, darling, but I don't feel that I can with this.' Rishaan's father was worried. When he had married Julia, they had both promised each other to help and support each other in their careers. Rishaan's mother was a journalist; it was her passion. Her independent spirit made her so attractive to him. Still, things were changing. It seemed that the world was getting crazier and more dangerous. The whole of Europe and the even the Middle East was sliding into chaos.

'Don't worry Richard,' she said, 'I'll be very careful.'

She knew what he was thinking. Julia had been near the Spanish village of Guernica when the Germans had bombed it during the Spanish Civil War. Her reports and photographs had made her a wanted person by Franco's nationalists, who had ordered the attack. Nonetheless, it was the death of Gerda Toro, the partner of the war photographer Robert Capa, which had worried Rishaan. Gerda was also a photographer, and following Capa's advice, 'If your pictures aren't good enough, you're not close enough,' she had gotten too close to the action at the battle of Brunete. In the retreat made by the republican army, a tank crushed the car she was in, and she died shortly afterward.

'I know you've been worried since Gerda died,' said Julia, holding her hand up to Rishaan's face. 'We knew them well. It was a shock for me—for all of us. We all felt it.'

'I remember how much Robert grieved at the funeral in Paris,' said Rishaan. 'It's a situation I don't want to be in, no matter how selfish you might think me to be.'

'I know. But remember my father. He was in so many wars since he was twelve, and he's still alive. And my mother never did a dangerous thing in her life, and she was killed in that tragic accident.'

'Yes, I must admit your family history does weaken my argument considerably. However, your grandfather now lives the life of a hermit, thinking his house is under siege from fictitious African warriors. He said it himself; he lost his courage when he lost your mother. If I lose you, I lose everything.'

Julia smiled. She knew she was demanding a lot, and she knew that Richard would be unhappy about her trip to the Middle East. 'If I make a promise that this will be the last trip, that after my confinement and the birth of our child I will only travel abroad when you are with me.' She put her hand on his thick black hair. He was still doubtful. 'The trip will only be for two weeks, and it's only to cover the immigration of Jews from Germany. It's not a war zone there.' He still did not look convinced.

'The Palestinians have been revolting against the British because they are not putting enough restrictions on the Jewish immigration. They are afraid the Jews will take all the better jobs and buy up all the land. It's a very difficult situation: the Jews are being persecuted in Europe, but when they go to their homeland, they are not allowed in. It's also unfair for the Palestinians. We British are not allowing them to have democratic elections and I want to find out why. Why are we scared of a democratic Arab government? It's a problem that's not going to go away, and I want to specialize in it as a journalist. But I will have no credibility if I have never been to Palestine.'

She put her hand on his face again; she loved his strong features and his Texan drawl. 'I'll be back before you know it, and you can be assured that this will be the last time.'

'I don't like this, Julia. I won't pretend to. I must think about Robert and Gerda. Of course, I won't stop you from going. The fact that you want to go is part of the reason I love you. But I'm not happy about it.'

Julia kissed him gently on the forehead, and they hugged.

Brian was pleased to see Rishaan and surprised to see Sam.

'Don't worry, Brian, Sam knows everything. I've told him.'

'Great spy you are. Is there anyone else in on the secret? Or anybody who isn't?'

'Well, I've got good news and bad news. I've managed to get the rest of the document...'

'Top notch!' shouted Brian.

'But my grandfather is also in on the secret. There was no other way.'

Brian frowned. 'Okay,' he said. 'But what does Sam here have to contribute?'

'Well Sam is my bodyguard. He was sent by my grandfather to keep an eye on the documents when they are in my possession. A good job, too, because they were nearly stolen by some pranksters.' Rishaan decided not to tell him the whole story.

Sam looked around him. 'Nice cat and mouse you 'ave 'ere,' he said.

'What?' asked Brian.

'He said it's a nice house,' translated Rishaan.

'Yes, it's our town pile. The family seat is Sandheim, in the sticks. I find that a foofaraw, but we allow father his peccadillo.'

'What?' asked Sam.

'He said his parents have their main house in the countryside. It's called Sandheim. It's a bit over the top.

'Built on a Jack and Jill, is it?' Sam asked.

Brian looked at Rishaan for a translation.

'Is it built on a hill?'

'No, in a valley. A bodyguard are you?' said Brian, looking Sam up and down. 'You've got the size, I'll give you that much, but I don't care much for braggadocio.' Brian stuck out his hand to shake Sam's hand.

Sam smiled and stuck out his hand as well, but Brian grabbed the upper side of his palm, twisted it, then turned into Sam, pulling him off his balance and then pushing and rolling him over his back so that Sam fell flat on the floor. It was done in an instant. Sam let out a whoosh as the air was knocked out of his lungs. There was a moment of silence as Sam picked himself up off the floor. Rishaan was flabbergasted; he didn't know what to do—whether to apologize to Sam, or castigate Brian, or to simply run.

'Blimey!' said Sam. 'Teach me how you do that!'

'It's easy,' said Brian. 'I've been studying Baguazhang; it's a Chinese martial art. I found an old book about it in the library. Fascinating! It's all about getting your assailant off his balance. Then it doesn't matter how big he is—in fact the bigger he is, the more his weight will work against him.'

Sam and Brian spent the next ten minutes throwing each other onto the floor. Rishaan had a go, but ended up landing on a pile of books, so he shrewdly left the two fighters to their fun. When Sam knocked over a table they decided to give it a rest, and Rishaan suggested they should work on the code.

'Yes, I agree, we have been obstreperous enough. I've been looking at the code. It's terribly hugger-mugger. A real olla podrida of words.'

'What did he say?' asked Sam, but Rishaan just shrugged his shoulders. Brian continued.

'I looked at the frequency of the letters in several books, and I made a graph of how many times all the letters of the alphabet are in a text. E is the most frequent, while Z is the least used. It's like Scrabble, really. It's funny, though, Ernest Hemmingway uses the letter E more than 'Practical Physics for Boys' does. I made a mistake trying to find the frequency. I forgot that the code is not in English, it's in German! And each language has its own frequency. For example, the letter E is even more frequent in German than English, by 17%. The J and the Y are seldom used in German. Anyway, I've got the frequency. Now the hard bit—we must establish the frequency in the document and map it to our German frequency.'

'Sounds like what my father does for a living. He's a safe cracker. He must decipher codes and combinations,' said Sam.

'Really? You mean like a burglar?'

'No, he's no tea leaf. He works for the government, does all sorts of jobs. Once he had to crack a safe at the Foreign office. They had lost the combination. Another time he had to open a safe they had recovered from a sunken submarine. He must open them without damaging the contents inside.'

'It's a pity we don't have the key,' said Brian. 'That would be our 'deus ex machina'. It's going to take a lot of counting and puzzling to figure out what's in the document.'

'That reminds me,' said Rishaan. 'Churchill said that my grandfather was the key, but we didn't know what that meant. My grandfather has a key-like scar on his arm. But how could that be the key?'

'What did he say, exactly?'

'He said that my grandfather was the key.'

'The word 'grandfather'? Or 'the grandfather of Rishaan Finch'?'

'No, he said that the sergeant major was the key.'

'So, the key could be the word 'sergeant major'.'

'I guess, but how would that help us?'

Brian scribbled out the alphabet on a piece of paper. Under the alphabet he wrote sergeant major, leaving out any letters that he had already used.

ABCDEFGHIJKLMNOPQRSTUVWXYZ

SERGANTMJOBCDFHIKLPQUVWXYZ

'This might be the key. It's a bit primitive—the chap that made the code was no expert—but it might work,' said Brian.

GAL ALPQNCUT GAL DA 209 V1 NSFG SF 1.
SUTUPQ 1938 PQSQQ WHEAJ PJRM ZAJTQA GSPP
GJA DSPRMJFA PAML PRMWAL ZU NCJATAN WSL

They scribbled it out on a piece of paper.

DER ERSTFLUG DER ME 209 V1 FAND AM 1.
AUGUST 1938 STATT, WOBEI SICH ZEIGTE, DASS
DIE MASCHINE SEHR SCHWER ZU FLIEGEN WAR.

'Perfect!' shouted Rishaan. 'You can already see regularity in the text. GAL is in there twice, while 'Der' is a very common German word. And I should have seen DA 209 meant the ME 209, which would have given us two letters straight away.'

'But what now? We've got nearly thirty pages of code to decipher – it's going to take ages,' said Sam.

'I thought of that,' said Brian, and he pulls a heavy metal object out of a box. 'My sine qua non!' he announced proudly.

'Wow, a typewriter. I've always wanted one of them,' said Sam. 'You rich kids have all the good stuff.'

'A 'Remington Deluxe noiseless' typewriter, to be precise,' countered Brian. 'If we change the letters around on the keys so that, for example, the letter A key types S and the letter B key types E, we just have to re-type the document, and it will decode itself!'

'Brilliant!' said Rishaan.

'But now that we have cracked the code, why don't we just give the documents back to Churchill, and let him get someone to decipher the text?' said Sam.

'Where's the fun in that?' asked Rishaan. 'Then we will never know what the text says.'

'But it's in German!' said Sam.

'Well, I speak German,' countered Rishaan.

'Churchill?' said Brian. 'Who said anything about Churchill?' He was alarmed.

'Good grief, it's impossible to keep a secret,' exclaimed Rishaan. 'Well, the documents are not my grandfather's; he got them from Churchill, who got them from a contact in Germany. It maybe evidence that the Germans are rearming.'

'This is jolly important!' said Brian. 'Any more secrets?' he asked. Rishaan told him about the incident on the underground. Brian laughed. 'Top notch! This is no time to be pusillanimous! Let's get to work!' declared Brian.

That night, as Rishaan lay in bed, he thought about his day and how exciting it had been. The idea that he was, albeit by accident, some sort of secret agent was to him something he felt he always wanted to do. It was part of him, as if he had been born to do it. Exciting, enthralling, dangerous—every emotion he could think of.

He had saved a woman's life, made friends with the son of a safe cracker, been robbed, and he had escaped invisible German agents and had cracked a secret code that might help a maverick politician to prove that a fascist country was preparing for war. Not a bad score for a twelve-year-old schoolboy.

However, he had done things wrong; he had inadvertently given away secrets. He had winged it. He had been lucky this time, but it was not something a true agent should do. It was stuff to think about as he drifted away into an exhausted sleep.

It was a few days later that they managed to translate the documents, and it made for sombre reading. It made several references to Jan Joseph Godfried, Baron van Voorst tot Voorst, a Dutch general who had been warning against

German rearmament before WWII. But most of the text was facts and figures. It included the locations of factories that the Germans were using to produce airplanes. It gave figures of production and a prognosis of how many planes the Nazis would have by 1940. It seemed like a lot, but Rishaan, Sam and Brian were no experts. The documents had been made secretly by a high civil servant within the German government, and there were several mistakes in the translation from German to the code. It had clearly been made quickly in secret. The general message, however, was clear. Rishaan made a conclusion of the text in English, which he put at the back of the documents, just in case Churchill would have trouble getting the work translated.

When it was finished, Rishaan rushed around to the sergeant major's and showed him the documents. The sergeant major looked at the pages for a long time, sipping his tea and looking serious. Finally, he drew his conclusion.

'It's in German,' said the sergeant major. 'You know what this means.'

'What?' said Rishaan, excited.

'It means I can't read it.' The sergeant major laughed out loud, making the mouse on the stuffed lion's head run away.

Rishaan told the sergeant major about the contents of the document, and he read the conclusion that he had made.

'You have to contact Churchill,' said Rishaan's grandfather. He seemed more serious now.

Rishaan didn't like going to the attic, but he knew he had no choice, so it didn't help thinking about it. He climbed the steps to the top, swung open the door and walked boldly over to the telephone. He picked up the receiver. Again, the ringing tone, which was then quickly answered by the same woman on the other end.

'Yes?'

Rishaan decided to keep it mysterious and ambiguous. 'Tell Churchill we have translated the document.'

'Yes, I will,' said the woman, and hung up.

So that was that. Rishaan left the documents and the decoded text with the sergeant major and then went home. It was still bitterly cold in London, so much so that despite his bad experience in the Underground, Rishaan took it again anyway. He knew had nothing to be afraid of; he no longer had any secret documents with him, but still, it made him nervous.

The next few days nothing much ensued. It was as if nothing had happened, so Rishaan started to prepare himself for his new school. The governess helped him with some things, mostly buying the right uniform and school supplies. Then one day Sam came around.

'Your grandfather wants to see you,' he said. The sergeant major had never sent for him, so it sounded very exciting. They both rushed off to Islington on the underground. Sam seemed a little quiet and he was constantly looking around.

'What does my grandfather want to see me for?' he asked.

Sam shrugged his shoulders. 'I don't know,' he said. 'He just gave me threepence to go and get you.'

Rishaan was worried. Maybe he had botched the decoding of the documents somehow; maybe they were too top secret for a couple of schoolchildren to have had in their hands. Somehow, he had the feeling he was in trouble. Sam was not giving anything away, but he certainly seemed on edge.

Rishaan's grandfather looked a bit concerned. 'Churchill came by the other day and picked up the documents. He was pleased with the result.' Rishaan knew there must be a problem.

'Churchill told me what he expected to find in the documents. I told him that I had not done the work, but you did,' said Grandfather. Rishaan groaned. Now there was going to be trouble; it was a good job they didn't know about the little adventure in the underground.

'Churchill brought you this,' he said, and he pulled out another envelope with documents in it. 'He said he needs them as quickly as possible.'

Sam smiled, and Rishaan was amazed, 'Great! Spiffing! Let's get onto it now!'

'Be careful if you take the Underground,' warned the sergeant major. 'When I was fighting in the trenches of the Great War, I was once buried underground by a mortar shell.' Rishaan's grandfather told him, wagging his finger. 'One of our own shells, as well—would you believe it? Took two days before the sappers could get anywhere near us. They had to wait until after the fighting had died down. Three of us were trapped in a small underground shelter, like rats in a sewer. In the beginning, we were right scared. Young lad with me nearly went mad, scrambling around, trying to dig out; he nearly made the whole shelter collapse. So I told him to listen carefully.

'What can you hear?' I asked him, talking smooth and relaxed, to calm him down.

'Nothing! Nothing, they've forgotten about us, they are not coming for us...'

'Listen again, son, listen. What do you hear?'

'So the boy listened, and he listened hard. 'I can hear gunfire, and bombs falling, and men screaming.'

'And what do you see?' So the boy looked around, in the dark shelter, lit by a candle; he tried to make out his entrapment.

'I see some tins of food, three bottles of brandy, some books...'

'I let him think a little, then I said, 'Tell me, boy, who are the ones that need rescuing?"

They took the underground back to Regents Park. On the way, Sam looked serious again, checking the people on the station and in the carriages. Rishaan held tightly onto the bag containing the documents. This is fun, he thought. I wonder what it's about. I wonder if anybody else knows about the documents, like last time.

'Let's get off at Oxford Circus,' whispered Sam, 'but then get back on the train again just as the doors are closing. That will confuse any people shadowing us.'

'Good idea,' said Rishaan.

They stepped off the carriage but just as they stepped back on again as the doors were closing, someone in the crowd on the platform pulled the bag off Rishaan's shoulder and ran off. The doors closed on them, trapping them in the carriage. Rishaan and Sam looked on helplessly as the train pulled out of the station. Sam, thinking quickly, pulled the emergency lever that stopped the train, throwing everybody forward. There were screams and insults as briefcases, newspapers and umbrellas flew. He then forced open the door and ran off in the direction of the thief. Rishaan was left in the carriage empty-handed. He decided not to stay and get any blame for pulling the emergency handle so he slipped off the carriage and left the station, walking the last few blocks to Brian's house at Regents Park. He doubled back a few times, then sneaked into Regents Park and climbed over the wall into Brian's garden.

'German agents , master Rishaan?' asked Tom the gardener.

'Funny you should say that, Tom, yes.'

'Fair enough,' replied Tom.

Rishaan found that Sam had already arrived before him. Both he and Brian looked frightened. 'What are we going to do?' asked Sam. He obviously had not been able to find the culprit. He looked as if he was about to burst into tears.

'Not much, but I don't think Grandfather will miss yesterday's newspapers,' said Rishaan, and from underneath his duffel coat, he pulled out the secret documents.

'You!' said Sam, pointing his finger at Rishaan. 'You! You...' he didn't seem to be able to say anything else.

'Trick me once, shame on you; trick me twice, shame on me,' said Rishaan.

Sam sat down; he was exhausted from the excitement and the chase. Brian grabbed the documents and set to work immediately.

'Well, obviously our last attempt was appreciated,' observed Brian. 'I'll try the same key as last time.'

'I think I had better get Sam a cup of tea,' said Rishaan.

Brian tried to decipher the document in the same way as before, but failed. 'It's not the same key,' he said. 'And looking at the paper and the typewriter and the way it's been made, I think it's by somebody else. It's been neatly typed and there are no corrections. The typewriter is of a higher quality, as is the paper. It's amazing how everything tells a story if you are willing to look and listen. If we can find out what kind of typewriter it was written on, and where the paper was made, that would tell us so many things, without even decoding the message.'

'I asked the sergeant major if there was a key, but he said there was not. I think that these are documents that have been stolen. These documents were not meant for Churchill's eyes. Look at the official stamps – that says GEHEIM, which means 'secret."

'Interesting!' said Brian, his eyes twinkling. 'The only way to decipher them, then, is to use frequency analysis. I assume it's in German, so let's use that.'

It was a lot harder than before. There were no numbers that would give away dates or known trademarks. Another problem was there were no words, just one long string of letters in blocks of four letters. Slowly, however, some words did start to appear, but they were not certain if they were a correct interpretation.

'I love a challenge,' said Brian, grinning from ear to ear like a Cheshire cat.

They seemed to be able to crack some words, but there were a lot of confusing changes.

'I think they have a double key,' said Brian. 'It makes it more difficult, but not impossible.'

'A double key?' asked Rishaan.

'It's like coding the message twice, with two different keys. We really need help from frequency analysis if that's the case.'

After a while, Rishaan decided he had better head home.

'I'm staying with the documents, even if it means sleeping here,' said Sam.

So Rishaan left them alone and went home. He felt strangely safe as he walked back to Kensington. He had nothing they could steal. One thing was sure now; somebody was out there and knew about the documents. But who was it, and what did they expect to discover?

Back at his house his mother was waiting for him. 'I've got a big surprise for you,' she said. 'I have been given an assignment with the Times newspaper to cover the events in Palestine. Your father has agreed to let me go to Palestine for a working visit for a few weeks, and I would like it if you came with me!'

'To Palestine? Excellent!' Rishaan was overjoyed. He loved traveling.

'Your Governess, Miss Dawkins, will come too. I've arranged that with the school, so you will have to do your homework and everything that Miss Dawkins tells you.'

'No problem, I've done this before; you know you can trust me. How are we going? By boat?'

'We will take the Ariberg Orient express to Athens, and from there we will take the ferry to Beirut, and drive down to Jerusalem.'

His father was examining and cleaning his pipe, so Rishaan knew he was unhappy.

'Are you coming too, Father?' asked Rishaan.

'I wish I could, but the embassy has bogged me down with too much work. I only conceded to let your mother go because I made her take you with her. You're the sensible one, Rishaan. You keep an eye on her; don't let her go climbing walls or scrambling down tunnels to get her blasted stories.'

He knew that his father was not happy with the prospect, so he tried his best to reassure him. 'You can rely on me father,' said Rishaan, as solemnly as he could. His father continued to vigorously clean his pipe.

Rishaan was very pleased. He had hardly known any other life than traveling in exotic lands. He knew when his father accepted the post at the embassy in London that those days were over for a while, so any chance he had to travel was gladly taken. It did clash, however, with his spying activities for Churchill. He could not tell his parents about this.

'When are we going?' he asked.

'In a few weeks. We will be gone about a month,' said his mother.

Superb, thought Rishaan. He could arrange something with Brian and Sam. Maybe they could decode the document before he went away.

Troops on the Move

THIS IS THE BBC CALLING:

At a meeting in Paris, French Foreign Minister Georges Bonnet met with Soviet Ambassador Jakob Suritz. They discussed that a 'peace front' comprising France, the Soviet Union, Great Britain, Poland and Romania would deter Germany from war.

Rishaan and Wouter visited the Natural History Museum and spent all day wandering around, marvelling at the fossils and stuffed animals. It had been a long day and it was getting late, they decided to leave. Wouter had many questions about the documents that had been decoded, but Rishaan tried to tell him only the minimum. Outside, Rishaan saw someone on the Cromwell road that he knew, and he was startled. It was Churchill. The politician had not seen him and was walking down the opposite side of the street. Wouter said he had to get home or his parents would be worried. He said goodbye to Rishaan and left, so Rishaan felt free to go over to Churchill and talk to him. He did not want to involve Wouter in a conversation with Churchill.

'Good day, Mr. Churchill.'

Churchill seemed lost in his thoughts and at first looked at the boy as if he didn't recognize him. 'Aha! My little code-cracker! What are you doing in Albertopolis?'

'Albertopolis?' asked Rishaan

'Yes, this area. They call it Albertopolis: you've got the Albert memorial, the Albert Hall, the Victoria and Albert...'

'I was at the Natural History Museum,' said Rishaan.

'It's a fine museum; I live across the road from it, here at number 41. That's when there are not too many small children around, and then I hide at my mother's home. You did a fine job on the document. I hope you are having the same success with my new assignment?'

'It's more difficult,' said Rishaan. 'We, er, I don't have a key to the code so it's more complicated. But it's not impossible; it just takes more time.'

'Speed is of the essence, my boy,' said Churchill. 'But don't think that I don't appreciate what you are doing for Britain.' And then, as an afterthought, he added, 'For the free world.'

'It will be ready next week,' said Rishaan. It had to be; he was going away the week after. 'I will be going away after that. Will there be more documents?' asked Rishaan.

'Oh, and where are you going?' asked Churchill.

'Palestine. My mother is a journalist. She is writing some articles on the problems the British are having there. My father says I must go, as well, to look after her. She can be a bit mad sometimes.'

'Indeed, interesting. Palestine is an exceptional problem. My good friend Lawrence of Arabia was a great fighter for that area. You should ask the sergeant major about him; they worked together. He died a few years ago in a motorbike accident. It's men like him that I need now in these turbulent times. Still, you may be of some use to me. Would you object if I ask you to take a package from me to a nice gentleman in Palestine? He will get in contact with you. All very hush-hush; don't tell anyone about it.'

'Of course,' said Rishaan, but he did not feel very comfortable about it.

'Excellent, now get along with your code breaking, boy. I've got my own problems – I do hope the children are not at home.'

As Churchill went up the steps to his house, Rishaan walked back to his own home. He preferred to walk; it gave him time to think about what Churchill had said. What was the package? It could be a bomb, or a gun, or more secret documents. And what if somebody else knew about the package? It was difficult enough getting the secret documents across London, let alone all the way to Palestine. Should he tell Churchill about the attempts to steal the documents on the underground? If Churchill found out, he would probably stop giving Rishaan documents to crack, and that would be a shame. It was like the sergeant major said: he enjoyed a challenge, being part of the battle.

The next day he visited Brian. Sam was there, and they had been working hard. They had managed to find some letters, but the words were German so they had difficulties spotting their successes and ignoring the failures. Every word had to be checked in a dictionary. It was a laborious process.

Rishaan buckled down to help them, working the typewriter and helping with the analysis. Slowly but surely, what seemed like coherent text finally started to emerge. Fortunately, the document was only a few pages. When they finally had finished, they were very pleased with their result. The content of the letter was the same as the previous document, but more formal and technical, like an inventory, stating specifics about machinery parts and the locations of factories. It was difficult to tell if this was of any help to

Churchill, or if it was even showing that Hitler was building an army.

When they were finished, Rishaan and Sam brought the documents back to the sergeant major. This time, Rishaan had a school bag which he clasped tightly to himself, while Sam had the real documents stuffed down his shirt.

'Mr. Churchill contacted me,' said the sergeant major, making another brew. 'He said that the package will be arriving the day before you leave, at 4 o'clock in the afternoon. He said you would understand.'

'Yes, er, it's two sugars in your tea isn't it, sergeant major?'

'Indeed it is.'

Rishaan wondered if he should tell the sergeant major that Churchill had asked him to take a package to Palestine, a secret package. Probably not a good idea, thought Rishaan. The sergeant major would not want to get into trouble with Rishaan's mother. Rishaan did not know if he knew that Julia was going to Palestine, so he did not want to get his mother into trouble with the sergeant major. Adults can be devilishly complicated sometimes, he thought.

There were no more documents to decode. Rishaan was glad in a way; he was worried about his next mission for Churchill. He would be traveling abroad with some secret package, and his mother would be with him. He would have to be very discreet. He decided to wait to see how big the package was, and maybe he could also figure out what it was.

Rishaan waited impatiently. His new school was interesting; there were lots of new friends to make. There were sons and daughters of ambassadors, important politicians, and many children from abroad, which Rishaan loved. He was always popular in this company because of his language skills. However, he felt detached and preoccupied. He was anxious about the coming trip.

Finally, the day before the trip, at 4 o'clock, the doorbell rang. Rishaan had been waiting, and he ran to the front door, shouting, 'I'll get it!'

What he found, he had certainly not expected. Standing in the cold of the London afternoon was a striking Indian girl and a large, fearsome servant with her baggage. He was huge man with a turban and a long beard and a long bejewelled knife stuck into his waistband.

'Hello,' she said. 'My name is Princess Anjuli Singh.'

She had beautiful skin and dark almond eyes. She had stunning dark brown pupils set in bright white. It was almost as if her eyes shone. Her skin was perfect, her hair silky and deep black. He could do little else but stare in wonderment. He had never seen such a wonderful creature. Rishaan was taken aback and was at a loss for words. She looked so special he did not even know if he was allowed to talk to her.

'Good afternoon Princess,' said Rishaan's mother, over Rishaan's shoulder, and she curtsied. 'Don't be rude Rishaan,' said his mother. 'It's not often a Princess comes visiting.'

Rishaan did the only thing he could think of and bowed. The Princess laughed and then waved at the limousine parked nearby. The chauffeur saluted and drove away.

'Please come inside, Princess Anjuli,' said Rishaan's mother.

The Princess had a fine bone structure and wore a sari that suited her elegant way of movement. The sari was long, and as she walked, she seemed to float along the marble floor. She was very curious about the house, looking around and asking questions about the pictures on the walls and the sculptures standing in the hall. The Indian soldier stood at attention at the doorway and would not budge.

'You have a beautiful house,' she said.

'Rishaan, this is Princess Anjuli and she will be accompanying us on our trip on the Orient Express. When we reach Athens, her uncle, Prince Mohammed Ali Singh, will accompany the Princess to the Punjab.'

This was a surprise to Rishaan. He was in any case relieved that the 'package' was not a bomb or a stolen secret dossier. In addition, he thought that Churchill said the package was to be delivered in Palestine. Still, he reasoned, things must often change in the clandestine world of spying.

'I see,' said Rishaan, still trying to find his composure. 'Well, I hope that we have a pleasurable time. I've heard that the Orient Express is a comfortable way to travel.'

'Thank you for allowing me to accompany you. My father, Prince Mohammed Allama, who is director of the Bank of Punjab, is inconvenienced with his business here in Europe. It is such a nuisance that the Germans are causing. There is so much instability and insecurity in the region. He seems to think I will be safer in India. From the news I've been hearing, I doubt if India is much better off.'

'Do you think there will be war in Europe?' asked Rishaan, plucking up his courage to talk to such a beautiful creature.

'Come now, Rishaan, where are your manners? It's not polite to interrogate a guest, especially royalty, particularly when they are hardly through the front door.'

The Princess smiled, and she was shown to her room by Julia. Later that evening the Princess's father arrived, and the two families had dinner together.

'Thank you so much for taking care of my Princess,' the father gushed. He was a large man, and he looked anxious and harried. Rishaan's father was curious about India's view on the problems in Europe.

'At the moment we have our own problems. Many Indians see the struggle in Europe as a weakening of the British influence on our continent, which it is. Some see it as a bad thing; others see it as an opportunity.'

'You mean Gandhi?' asked Rishaan.

'Gandhi is a very powerful man in India. He is a good man because he insists on non-violence, but he has a difficult position trying to keep India together. He would like very much for India to be independent of the British. He wants Swaraj, self-rule—for India to be a nation. However, many internal problems need to be resolved. Gandhi wants a peaceful change, but he is a small, frail man stopping many millions of people who want to fight. For example, Anjuli and I are Muslim. However, there are many Hindus in India; there are Muslims and Hindus that will not live together. It is a human tragedy that people fear the unknown, and therefore the uneducated have a great deal to fear. I fear the developments in Europe will result in the collapse of India, as we now know it—maybe even disintegration into anarchy. That would have consequences for the whole world.'

'America is aware of these problems,' said Rishaan's father, 'but there is little we can do about it. Britain would take a dim view if we were to meddle in its foreign affairs, especially as we're taking a neutral stance toward Hitler.'

'What is your opinion about Swaraj?' asked Rishaan.

The prince looked troubled.

'You must excuse my son,' said Rishaan's father. 'He is too direct and has too much curiosity.' Rishaan's father smiled. He was always surprised at the openness and inquisitiveness of his son, just as much as he was surprised at the direct and honest answers he got from his victims. He put it down to a potent combination of a strong intellect and a child's innocence. Rishaan caught the Princess looking at him, and he blushed.

'And it's a good question,' the Prince replied. 'I must ask myself - is Swaraj good for India and—I must admit more importantly, as a businessman—is Swaraj good for me? Is Swaraj good for India? If a magic wand waved over India and bestowed the wisdom of Gandhi on everybody, I would say yes. Morally and psychologically, a country, especially one as large as India, must be free from foreign domination, no matter how benevolent. However, young Rishaan, the devil is in the details.'

'Is Swaraj good for me?' he continued. 'I have a blessed and rich life; my prosperity, the way I care for my family, is based on the status quo as it is now. There is a saying, if it's not broken, don't fix it. I don't think India is broken. If the power structure changes in India, I might lose what I have, and this is not good for me, or my family.' He looked at his daughter, who has gone to sit with Rishaan's mother by the fire, and he smiled.

Rishaan was disappointed that Anjuli had left and was torn between listening to the Prince or joining her.

'There are a great many people in India who do not have what I have and may find a way in an unstable situation to take that from me. I, too, Rishaan, fear the unknown. As a father and a businessman, my life is about risk.' Rishaan could see that the prince was worried.

Rishaan's mother called him over to come and sit with them. Rishaan was interested in the Princess's opinion, but he knew that his mother was calling him so that he would leave his father to discuss something with the prince. Maybe it was something about the Princess. She was indeed a unique creature. She was maybe a year younger than Rishaan was, and had an accent that betrayed that she was not brought up in England. However, she was obviously comfortable in a well-to-do environment and being a Princess gave her a special quality that made Rishaan slightly bashful, something he was not used to. Or was it because she was a beautiful girl?

'Sit here, Rishaan, next to the fire, and I will go and get Cook to bring some milk and biscuits.'

Rishaan sat next to the fire. Anjuli looked especially pretty in her sari next to the radiance of the hearth. The light from the fire glowed on her tanned skin and jet black hair. Rishaan smiled at her; she smiled back with her dark almond eyes, making Rishaan very nervous.

'What languages do you speak?' asked Rishaan.

'Well, English, of course,' said Anjuli. 'My mother language is Urdu, which is the language I use when I am in India. I understand a lot of Punjabi. The written language of Punjabi and Urdu is the same. Urdu is the most common language, especially among the elite.'

Rishaan smiled; Anjuli was definitely one of the elite. She said 'elite' in an easy way that did not betray any arrogance or self-importance. It was just the way it was; it was what she was used to. Rishaan had travelled enough to see poverty and deprivation, albeit from the train window, or traveling in a car through the bustling streets of Khartoum. He assumed that Anjuli had also seen poverty in the streets of Delhi and the Punjab.

'I have never heard any Urdu. Is it a difficult language to learn?'

'Urdu grammar can be very complex and is dissimilar in many ways to English. For example the verbs usually fall at the end of the sentence rather than before the object. And we don't have the word 'the'.'

Rishaan's mother returned with the biscuits and milk.

'I'm going to try and get Anjuli to teach me Urdu,' announced Rishaan.

'Oh Rishaan, you are such a nuisance,' said his mother.

'Well, we can start by not saying the word 'the',' said Anjuli, 'and putting the verbs at the end.'

'Agreed,' said Rishaan. There then followed a silence which made them both giggle.

Rishaan felt a closeness to the Princess he had never felt before, as if he had known her forever. Yet he had only just met her. He felt confused, but intrigued. He was glad she was going with them on the train trip; he would have the chance to talk to her more.

The next day, while packing his belongings for the trip, his mother gave him some extra news. 'We have an additional traveller with us, Jan Jágr. You may remember him from our stay in Munich. His father is a minister for the Czechoslovakian government. His father has asked us if Jan can travel with us as far as Budapest.'

'I don't remember the name, but I might remember the face,' said Rishaan.

'He will be with his valet, as will Anjuli. Yes I know, it is turning into a bit of a circus, but the good news is your governess will be joining us later, so we will have each other to ourselves for the first week in Palestine.' His mother smiled at him.

'Yes!' shouted Rishaan. His mother was often busy, and to have her all to himself for a week was great.

'But you will still have to do your homework, young man, I will see to that.'

Rishaan did not mind, and he did not mind Anjuli and Jan joining him, as well. Soon the house was alive with valets and baggage, maids, butlers and chauffeurs.

Rishaan's father stood around, cleaning his pipe. He was not happy and was snapping at the help.

'You take good care of your mother,' he said, pointing his pipe at Rishaan. 'And take good care of yourself. And you take good care of Rishaan,' he said to Julia, frantically wiping his pipe.

'Yes,' said Julia, 'we will all take good care of each other.'

'You can rely on me, Father,' said Rishaan, but his father did not look convinced.

Jan arrived shortly, Rishaan did not remember him but they soon became friends. Jan spoke reasonable English, but excellent German, which was not a problem for Rishaan. They conversed in a mix of the two languages, flipping back and forth in whatever language expressed itself better. However, they did not have much time to talk, as the baggage was ready and everybody, including Anjuli's Sikh bodyguard, was off to their first stop, Paris. Rishaan's father waved to the entourage as it sped off toward Victoria Station. He still looked worried, but Julia looked energized and thrilled. She was off on an adventure, just like the old days!

As the train raced across the snow-covered English countryside towards Dover, the children and Rishaan's mother had their own cabin in first class, while the servants were in the coaches. The Sikh bodyguard wandered around in the corridors, eyeing everybody suspiciously and making the women in second class nervous. Anjuli and Rishaan's mother settled down to read, so Rishaan and Jan talked in German.

'I was sent by my father to a private boarding school in Oxford.' said Jan. 'He thought I would pick up English faster that way, which I guess is true, but I didn't like it there. The other students heard me speaking German and that is not popular now, after the Great War. I tell them I am Czech, but it makes no difference. My father decided to bring me back, and I am so grateful. I may be sent to a private school in Prague, but that depends a lot on the situation. The Germans are threatening to take the Sudetenland; we're all a bit wary of what Hitler has plans for next. Hitler is good at stirring up differences between people, and Czechoslovakia has many differences: German speakers, Slovaks, Czechs, even Poles. We've had a lot of ethnic problems.'

Jan had black hair and hazel eyes; he was the same size and age as Rishaan. He seemed weary of his trip to England and was glad to be getting back to his home land.

'My father is worried about the future. Hitler is a madman with crazy notions about race. In our country there are many different types of races and religions. Take me, for example:

my family is from the Bohemian province, but some people on my mother's side are ethnic Slovaks; my great-grandfather was a gypsy; a grandmother on my father's side was Jewish. My mother's sister married a Hungarian; my father's sister married a German speaker. It's all very confusing and frightening when you hear that Hitler is deporting populations just because of their ethnicity.'

'It's a sad world when twelve-year-old boys are talking about ethnicity,' said Rishaan's mother, and smiled at Jan. 'Oh, why do I always feel the cold?' she said, and wrapped herself up in more blankets.

They arrived in Paris on schedule and they took taxis to the Hôtel Ritz. Their luggage was kept at the station, ready for their early departure after a day's stay in Paris. Rishaan loved the Hôtel Ritz. It had lots of passageways and corridors and after the long journey he, Anjuli and Jan were keen to stretch their legs.

They wandered around; everybody seemed to be rich and important. 'Isn't that Charlie Chaplin?' asked Jan. There was a ballroom and conference rooms. There seemed to be grand pianos everywhere, and large bay windows opening out onto perfectly-kept gardens.

They entered the main restaurant. It was glamorous, with mirrored walls, gold-plated statues and silver buckets containing champagne, and there was a constant hum of merry French conversation. In one of the corners there was a group of people who seemed to be merrier than the rest. They had popped champagne and were drinking toasts to anything absurd they could think of.

Someone in the group proposed a toast to 'giraffes', which was greeted with much delight.

'That's Pablo Picasso, the famous painter,' whispered Anjuli. 'My father was going to buy one of his paintings for the Bank in London, but my mother made him buy a Modigliani instead.'

Then one of the group stood up, a short man in a dark suit with a fez. He looked Egyptian. 'I propose a toast to that beautiful Indian girl in a sari,' he offered, and they all raised their glasses to Anjuli.

'She's not only beautiful; she's also a Princess,' said Rishaan in Arabic.

The Egyptian was impressed. 'Well! Well! A western boy speaking Arabic! I think I've had enough champagne for today!' They all laughed.

Picasso asked Anjuli a question, but she could not speak French.

'I'm afraid my friends do not speak French,' said Rishaan, apologetically. 'The Princess is on her way to India, from London.'

'A Princess indeed,' said another man, dressed in a French army uniform, and they all toasted that as well.

'If I hear correctly, your French is good but you have an English accent,' said Picasso.

'If I hear correctly, your French is good but you have a Spanish accent,' said Rishaan in Spanish, much to the amusement of the group. Rishaan liked showing off.

The group invited Rishaan and his friends to join them, but Anjuli and Jan were not enthusiastic, especially as the champagne was flowing freely and the air was blue with cigarette smoke. There was something about adults behaving like children that made the children nervous. Anjuli said she was tired, and Jan said he wanted to read, so they all made their excuses and left.

Rishaan still had too much energy, so he roamed the corridors of the Ritz, looking at all the beautiful objects and interesting people around him.

In one of the corridors there were several paintings hanging on the wall. They were all different in style and subject. One was of a woman holding a guitar. She was painted as if she was flat, she had one eye and her nose was painted on the side of her head. Her skin had a sickly green colour and the background was split up into irregular shapes. The guitar was disjointed, and in some places, bits of newspaper had been added. Rishaan could make neither head nor tail of it.

'Do you like it?' asked Picasso, giving Rishaan a surprise.

'She's not very beautiful,' said Rishaan. 'If I were to paint a woman I would paint a beautiful one.'

This made Picasso laugh. 'That is my wife,' he said.

'Sorry,' said Rishaan. 'But I'm sure she doesn't look like that.'

'If I wanted to have a realistic picture of my wife, I would take a photograph. But then again, my wife is not two inches tall, two-dimensional, and with no colour but only shades of grey.'

'I guess not, I've never met her,' said Rishaan, which made Picasso laugh.

'You should look at this painting as many small expressions of emotion put together. Each bit is an image or part of an object from the left, from the right. From any angle the artist pleases—he has that freedom. Each detail is an homage to something that the artist likes about the subject. Each bit tells a story. It's like a picture in code.'

'So you could send coded messages to your friends disguised as pictures of a woman playing guitars?' asked Rishaan. That intrigued him.

'Well, I had not thought of it that way, but I guess you could,' laughed Picasso. 'I painted a picture about the Spanish Civil War and I put some hidden imagery in that. But I want people to feel my paintings, not have to decipher them.'

'There you are, Rishaan. I've been looking all over for you,' said Rishaan's mother. 'And good day, Mr. Picasso,' she said in French, and Picasso kissed her hand.

'I'm honoured to meet you,' she gushed. 'I saw your painting Guernica in London. I was very impressed. I was near Guernica when they bombed it, working as a journalist. It was a great tragedy.'

'Indeed, I trust you have heard the news. Today France and England have recognized Franco's Spain.'

Rishaan's mother was taken aback. 'I was afraid that would happen, after Franco took Barcelona, but Madrid is still in republican hands.'

'It is only a matter of time,' said Picasso. Rishaan's mother looked sad.

'Excuse me,' said Picasso, 'my friends will be missing me. Have a pleasant stay in Paris.' He kissed Rishaan's mother's hand again and left. Rishaan could see that his mother was troubled by the news she had just heard but knew that this maybe was not the right time to start asking questions. She looked as if she needed to come to terms with it herself first.

'It's time to retire,' said his mother. 'We have had a long day, and the day after tomorrow we have a long journey ahead of us.'

The next day Rishaan left his mother to meet her friends and walked around Paris on his own. Princess Anjuli went with his mother, as Julia had promised her that they could go to some shops. Rishaan and Jan took off on their own. Rishaan took his camera with him and they walked around the Sacre Coeur, Montmartre and Montparnasse, ending up reading books at a bookshop called Shakespeare and Company.

Rishaan saw a trip to Versailles. He had never been there before, but Jan was tired so they split up. Rishaan took the bus to Versailles to look around the Palace there. On the way back he saw a crowd outside one of the buildings in town and a strange wooden contraption that pointed upward. The crowd seemed hostile and there seemed to be something about to happen.

'What's going on?' Rishaan asked a lady, in French, who had some small children with her.

'That's Eugen Weidmann,' she said, pointing to man in a white shirt who was being escorted out from a building. He had his hands behind his back. 'A terrible man – he kidnapped and murdered several people. He murdered a beautiful young American girl whom he lured to his home. He shot five people! He's not the smartest of crooks though. One of his victims took photographs of them together and he left the camera next to the body.'

As soon as Weidmann appeared the crowd began to call and shout, and the few police officers who were attending started to look very nervous. They took Weidmann and placed him on what looked like a table, next to the wooden scaffolding, and it was then that Rishaan realized it was a guillotine.

They spent some time fiddling with the guillotine, and they had to pull him off the table to adjust something. The crowd seemed to get angrier, and Rishaan thought that they might even try to lynch the man. The man would be executed, they reassured the crowd, trying to keep them back. The crowd had smelt blood and wanted satisfaction.

Rishaan took some photographs, but a police officer came over to him and told him to stop. It was against the law, the officer said.

Rishaan's heart pounded. He had never seen anybody being executed before. It was a strange feeling to know that here was someone, no matter who it was or what he had done, someone alive who would soon die. The man now faced death and nobody was going to help him. Rishaan could only think of stopping something like this happening, like stopping an accident or helping someone who was hurt. But to deliberately kill someone? It seemed so clinical and unfeeling. The man was helpless; his hands were handcuffed behind his back. Rishaan could see his face. He looked scared, but somehow accepting and passive, even drugged. He looked at the crowd as they booed and cajoled.

Rishaan knew that this was not a good man. He had committed those crimes, he had confessed, but this still seemed barbaric. Suddenly, the man in the white shirt was grabbed and placed on the table again. A holding block was quickly placed around his neck and immediately the knife noisily slipped down the frame and sliced his head from his body. The body was quickly rolled over into the coffin that was placed next to the table, and the head was tossed into the coffin after it. A cheer went up from the crowd and it surged forward, kept back only by the commands of the police.

Rishaan felt sick to his stomach. He felt dirty and guilty about being a spectator to this man's death. This was not a punishment, he thought, this was entertainment. He decided he didn't want to see any more and left Versailles to go back to Paris. He hated the way people treated each other. Although some guilty people murder innocent people, do innocent people kill murderers? Did it have to be like that?

On the way back, some of the people from the crowd were on the bus. Two people were laughing.

'It was a wild crowd at this one!' said the old lady in the black dress.

'Yes,' said the old man next to her, 'Weidmann was not the only one who lost his head,' and they sniggered.

'Anyway,' said the woman, 'that's one German less to bother us French.'

The man nodded in agreement.

Rishaan felt bad. Yet the people around him all seemed to be in a party mood. Was he so different from them? Had his privileged background made him more civilized? They seemed to enjoy the suffering and death of a human being. It did not matter who he was. Rishaan wanted to know why, to understand it.

He felt afraid of the people on the bus; they seemed like a different species to him. He thought some of them had spotted him, were watching him, ready to pounce. Some looked evil.

Maybe it was because the prisoner was a German. Many French people had lost loved ones during the recent World War with Germany. Maybe the old man and woman in front had lost a son.

When he arrived back in Paris he went straight to the Hotel and hugged his mother. He was grateful for who he was and the special life he had. It made him feel strong, but at the same time strangely vulnerable and alienated.

The next day, it was chaos from the moment Rishaan's mother woke him. There were servants and maids and valets and butlers. Even Anjuli's bodyguard, who did nothing more than stand around looking menacing, got in the way. Everybody was finally herded into taxis and they were off to the Gare de l'Est.

'The train leaves at 10.15, children, hurry, hurry!' Rishaan's mother cajoled the group.

They just made the train. An old friend of Rishaan and his parents, Lt. Wordsworth, was also taking the train, and he helped Rishaan and the other travellers hurry aboard. They were still searching for their cabin when the train was pulling out of the station. As the train travelled through the suburbs of Paris, Rishaan witnessed the same poverty that surrounds all major cities.

Rishaan knew it would be useless to ponder it too much. The train was gathering speed and yet there was still poverty outside. There were miles and miles of poverty. There were dark shabby houses where people lived and miserable industrial buildings where the same people worked. It was the same on the outskirts of London and in the industrial centres around Washington and New York. The cold, grey winter sky was the same colour as the smoke coughing from the factory chimneys.

The black and leafless trees stood silhouetted in the murky polluted snow. Finally, the urban landscape started to disappear as the train struggled free and the scene changed into fields and farms. He did not know if the farmers were as poor as the city dwellers, but it looked like a cleaner, healthier poverty.

Rishaan thought about what he wanted to do with his life. He decided he wanted to make everybody rich and happy, but he was not quite sure how. He would like to be a lawyer and defend people like prisoner Weidmann, even though he was a bad person.

He did not like sitting still for too long. Neither did Jan, so they went off to explore the train. It was a hotchpotch of different carriage models from all over Europe. There was a Swiss coach, two Hungarian coaches, and a Viennese restaurant coach. Several German and French First Class coaches made up the collection. Their fellow passengers were as assorted as the rolling stock they were traveling in.

'We have a mutual friend,' said Jan, when they were alone.

'Yes, who?' asked Rishaan.

'My father knows Winston Churchill,' said Jan. 'He arranged for me to travel with you. My father said that Winston spoke highly of you.' Rishaan was taken aback. He had obviously been confused about which package Churchill was talking about.

Jan became very serious. 'Churchill told my father that you were to be trusted. He said that you had helped him before and that you might be useful to us.' Rishaan was afraid that his mother might overhear what Jan was saying; he really wanted to keep it a secret.

'Don't worry, this is just between you and me,' said Jan. They moved down the carriages until they found an empty cabin. Jan was nervous, and he whispered, looking around furtively. 'One of my relatives is a Polish man, Marian Rejewski. He works for the Polish intelligence, the department that deciphers messages, the Biuro Szyfrów. They have found out through a spy at the German intelligence that the Germans have developed a cipher machine that is almost impossible to break. It's some sort of machine that works like clockwork, with cogs and springs. My relative might have found a way of cracking the code using mathematics; it's all very complicated. He is not ready yet, but he is close. The Polish government is communicating with the British but my relative thinks that both governments are playing down the importance because they are trying to appease Germany. They are hoping that Hitler might undo himself of his own accord. Hitler is such a lunatic, everybody hopes that his own people will overthrow him. Some people think that Churchill is our only hope, but he is also regarded as a warmonger. My relative is forbidden to communicate with anyone, especially not with someone like Churchill, but he believes that if he cracks the code Churchill should at least understand what is going on.'

'This sounds great,' said Rishaan. 'Is there anything I can do to help?'

'My father has asked me to keep in contact with you. We're not too suspicious, just two schoolboys, practicing their German and their English, as pen pals.'

Rishaan did not understand at first how being pen pals would help, but it quickly dawned on him. 'So you will be writing in code!' said Rishaan, full of enthusiasm.

'Shush!' said Jan. 'Yes. I know nothing about codes but Mr. Churchill said that you were an expert; you would tell me how.'

It was a good question. 'Let me think about it. I'll let you know before you get off at Budapest.'

They went back to the cabin were Rishaan's mother and Princess Anjuli were. Rishaan thought about the coded pen pal letter. He could use a key, like the first coded document he had deciphered. But that message was clearly in code, and if intercepted would be very suspicious. Then Jan and his family would be in a lot of trouble. However, Jan's English was bad enough to fake spelling mistakes, so that could be used to his advantage. But how?

The train started to snake its way through the lower hills and smaller mountains of the Alps.

Rishaan's mother was reading, and Jan and Princess Anjuli had fallen asleep, covered in some fur coats.

Then a thought struck Rishaan. Maybe Princess Anjuli was the 'package' Churchill was talking about, after all. Maybe he wanted Rishaan to keep in contact with her as well, as a pen pal, the perfect way to covertly pass messages. However, she had not mentioned Churchill. With Jan it was clear what the advantage was and the messages that Jan would be able to communicate with Churchill. Jan was also different in that he had his family involved.

Was sending Jan with Rishaan Churchill's way of inspiring Rishaan to get the Princess involved without her or her family knowing about it? Churchill was very interested in the problems in India that would arise for the British if Britain was involved in a European war. It would make sense for him to have an innocent ear in the courtyards of the Punjab. Oh, that's clever, thought Rishaan, very clever indeed.

With the gentle rocking of the train, Rishaan soon fell asleep. Suddenly the train jerked to a halt. Rishaan awoke with a shock and looked outside. Soldiers in strange uniforms ran down the sides of the carriages, Rishaan thought that they were going to board the train, even arrest them for spying. But they rushed on past and ran toward another train that was just pulling in from the other direction. The soldiers swarmed all over the train, and soon, some refugees were pulled out from underneath the carriage. There were three of them; they looked very young. They were almost blue from the cold and soaking wet. Rishaan's mother turned them away from the window.

'They are probably Jews,' said Jan. 'They are trying to escape from Austria. We're in Switzerland now.'

'What will happen to them?' Rishaan's mother asked Jan.

'They will probably be sent back. Switzerland is very, how you say, 'behutsam'?'

'Careful,' translated Rishaan.

'Yes, careful, of their neutrality.'

The Jewish youths looked frightened. They were dirty and tired.

Before Rishaan could stop her, Rishaan's mother disembarked and ran out onto the train siding and tried to go over to the youths where their captors where holding them. The train conductor came over and stopped her, insisting that she re-board the train. Rishaan admired her for her courage, but he knew, as she probably feared, that it was hopeless. Rishaan's mother returned to the carriage, obviously upset about the event, and as their train began to pull out of the station, she opened the window and waved at the youths.

'Good luck!' she shouted, but they seemed too traumatized to react.

As the train sped on from Zurich to Innsbruck and Vienna, Rishaan wondered what more he was going to see of the effects of Hitler and his fascists.

His mother stared out of the window for a long time, watching the fields of Switzerland grow and swell slowly into the mountains of Austria. She seemed lost in her thoughts. Her book lay on her lap, but she did not read a page. After a while she gathered the children together.

'I want to tell you a little about the Jews,' she said. 'This is important for you, Rishaan, as we're going to Palestine, but it's also important for you, Anjuli and Jan, as it's a part of the problems in Europe that I fear we will be experiencing for some time to come.'

Rishaan settled down to listen; he loved it when his mother talked about history. She had the same way of telling stories as her father, the sergeant major.

'The ancient Israelites lived in the area called the Fertile Crescent,' she said. 'This is the area lying between the Nile River in Egypt on the one side, and the Tigris and the Euphrates rivers in Iraq on the other. The civilizations of Egypt and Babylon and the deserts of Arabia and the highlands of Asia Minor surrounded their region.

'This expanse, later known as Israel, then at various times Judah, Coele-Syria, Judea, Palestine, and the Levant, had important harbours on the Mediterranean coast and the Gulf of Aqaba.'

Rishaan's mother pulled out an old Atlas, probably a present from the sergeant major, and opened it to a map of the Middle East. She showed the general area, pointing to the major rivers and the lands of Turkey and Persia.

'There were many travellers in this area,' she continued, 'passing from Europe to Asia, following trade routes, selling and buying goods. It was a mix of many cultures and civilizations. The ancient Israelites traced their ancestry to Abraham, an important prophet for the Christians, Jews and Muslims. Jewish tradition holds that the Israelites are the descendants of Abraham's grandson, Jacob. Jacob had twelve sons who settled in Egypt. Their descendants divided into twelve tribes, but they were enslaved under the rule of Ramses II. The prophet Moses led the exodus of the Israelites from Egypt to escape this enslavement.

'The twelve tribes wandered in the deserts of Arabia for forty-one years before finally settling in Canaan. That's how the nation of Israel was born. The tribes were ruled by judges until it was turned into a monarchy by Saul, which was later ruled by David and Solomon. After Solomon died the kingdom split into two, Israel and Judea. Israel was overrun by the Assyrian ruler Shalmaneser V; Judea was conquered by an Iraqi army. There was always trouble in the area, with civil wars and invasions from foreign forces, among them Alexander the Great. Worse was to come. A Roman campaign of conquest, led by Pompey, soon followed. Judea under Roman rule was at first a Jewish kingdom, but soon they came under the direct rule of a Christian administration. This was a cruel and violent government and the Jews revolted. The uprising was defeated by the Romans, who destroyed much of the Temple in

Jerusalem. In the second century Julius Severus ravaged Judea and banished the Jews from Jerusalem altogether.

'Many Jews were sold into slavery; others became citizens of other parts of the Roman Empire. It was official policy to convert any remaining Jews to Christianity, whether they liked it or not.

'The Battle of Yarmouk was the first great wave of Muslim conquests outside Arabia and was a forerunner for the advance of Islam into Christian Palestine, Syria and Iraq. Many Jews who had fled the cruelty of the Roman Empire returned to the area under the protection of the Muslim Caliphate, preferring the gentle intolerance of the Arabs to the outright killing suffered under Christian rule. The Jews even defended Jerusalem and Haifa with the Muslims against the Christians in 1099 during the first crusade. Jews were regularly massacred or exiled from various European countries as a result. Thriving communities on the Rhine and the Danube were destroyed. In 1147 the Jews in France were subject to frequent massacres. English Jews were banished; 100,000 Jews were expelled from France; thousands were expelled from Austria. Many of these expelled Jews fled to Poland.'

'My grandfather is a Polish Jew,' said Jan. 'There are a lot of Jews in Poland.'

'Well, that's no thanks to the Cossack Chmielnicki, who massacred hundreds of thousands of Jews, and the Jews killed in the Swedish wars,' replied Rishaan's mother.

Princess Anjuli put her arm around Rishaan's mother's arm and leaned against her shoulder. Rishaan's mother seemed to realize that maybe her story was a bit too serious for the innocent ears of a Princess; maybe she had better water it down a little. Sometimes she forgot they were just children.

'From 1700 onward there was a period of enlightenment. Jews were no longer banned or forced to live in Ghettos. The French revolution gave freedom to Jews as individuals; Napoleon was one of the great Jewish liberators, protecting them under law. However, individual freedom was not enough. A Jew was allowed to be a Jew, but their traditions were not tolerated. This gave birth to Zionism.'

'What's Zionism?' asked Rishaan, but his mother did not have a chance to answer. The cabin door slammed open and a uniformed soldier stormed in. His oiled leather jacket, brown shirt, leather boots and riding trousers gave a very menacing appearance. He had a trimmed moustache, made popular by Adolf Hitler, and close-cropped hair.

'Pass, bitte!' he barked. Rishaan's instinct was to get between his mother and the intruder, but the guard pushed him to one side. It happened so quickly, but his mother intervened swiftly, telling Rishaan to keep still, and she calmly reached for her bag to retrieve the documents. The guard made a few notes, eyeing everybody suspiciously, especially Rishaan. There was something about the man; he did not seem like a guard. He was strong, physically trained. He had been in some sort of accident; there was a scar on his face. It seemed almost as if one eye was damaged; maybe it was even a false eye. There was another thing: covered under his coat he had a jacket, which had two collar tabs. They were dark yellow with the symbol of a young eagle with one claw on a swastika. Rishaan thought it a bit strange, since they were in Austria. It was an odd collar tab for a border guard. His accent was also wrong.

It did not have the soft Austrian tones, but it was difficult for Rishaan to check, as the man did not say much. The guard turned to leave, but the Princess's bodyguard, who did not look at all pleased, growled, blocking his way. He stood a full six inches above the Austrian and glared with all his might and beard at the now-dwarfed civil servant. His hand rested on his bejewelled Talwar sword, tucked into his waistband.

'Tell Singh to let the gentleman pass,' whispered Rishaan's mother to Princess Anjuli, and Anjuli obliged in Urdu. The giant Indian soldier reluctantly stepped out of the way, and the guard slithered past and departed.

That was strange, thought Rishaan. He also saw how frightened Jan had been of the guard. He had gone very white and sat in the corner of the carriage, wide-eyed.

Rishaan's mother had Jan come over and sit next to her. 'Anyway, I was telling you about Zionism,' she said, trying to divert the subject, but she changed her mind. 'Yes, well, I think maybe another subject than that. Let me think. Yes! Let me tell you about that charming Lt. Wordsworth whom we met at the train station. I'll ask him to dine with us tonight, so he will confirm my story.

'Anyway, Lt Wordsworth is a friend of the family. He's a cousin of George Mainlin, Rishaan, and they own Franley House—you've been there. Lt. Wordsworth almost married Lord Cheltmine's daughter, Beverly. Yes, well, that means nothing to you, I'm sure. It was quite the drama at the time. He had to hide at our house, Chelmsford Hall, for two months to let things die down. He is the reason the statue of Pan in the fountain at Chelmsford Hall is leaning a bit to the left. He arrived home drunk one night and crashed his car into it. He had the audacity then to tell Ambrose the Butler to park the car.

'Anyway, Lt. Wordsworth was in the Air Force serving in Africa. His first campaign was to explore the possibility of air power in British Somaliland in the Horn of Africa. A Muslim cleric called Mohammed bin Abdullah, although we all called him the 'Mad Mullah', had gathered around him a large band of armed followers. The local colonial administration was trying to establish law and order but was being stopped by these insurgents, and their frustration was reaching London. The colonial office was demanding military action against this Mad Mullah but the government was a bit wary. The British Army had estimated that it would cost three divisions of soldiers and at least several million pounds. This was just after the Great War, so public opinion was very much against new military actions, as it still is with 'Mad Hun Hitler'. Anyway, the foreign office was in a conundrum at what to do. Along comes Viscount Trenchard, who's trying to keep his newly founded Royal Air Force free from the army.

'Gentleman,' he says, at his club in London, puffing on his big cigar, 'give me £100,000 sterling and I will take care of this 'Mad Mullah' for you'. So off they went, Lt. Wordsworth and his fellow officers and their de Havilland DH9s, and they spent the next few weeks buzzing the Mad Mullah like bees after nectar. They chased the insurgents all the way back to their stone forts. They called it the cheapest war in history. Churchill was colonial secretary at the time. He told me he was so impressed with the success of the control from the air that he used the same policy to bring stability to Iraq.'

'I didn't know Hugh Trenchard smoked cigars,' said Rishaan.

His mother laughed. 'Artistic license, darling. I was being metaphorical.'

Jan seemed to have cheered up a bit. 'Will we meet him at dinner?' Jan asked, excited. 'I hope to be a pilot one day as well!'

'May I go find him and ask?' asked Rishaan.

'Yes, you may, Rishaan, but don't be demanding. If Lt. Wordsworth wishes to be left alone this evening then it's up to him. He is a bit of a gadabout so he might not have the time for socializing with the likes of us. I'm sure he has more interesting things to do.'

Rishaan went looking for the lieutenant. He assumed that he would be traveling first class, but he found him in one of the second-class carriages, snoozing. A book lay on his chest and a hip flask on the ledge rocked slightly with the movement of the train.

'I've been looking all over for you,' said Rishaan. The lieutenant opened one eye and looked at the boy. The pilot seemed to come from a deep sleep, and he looked at Rishaan for a few seconds as if he did not recognize him.

'Oh, yes, you're Julia Finch's boy,' he said finally, wiping his face with his hands to wake himself up. 'Are we there yet?' he asked, looking out of the window, trying to make sense of the mountains outside.

'You're a pilot! Spiffing!' said Rishaan, but the pilot didn't seem to share the boy's enthusiasm.

The pilot put the book to one side and took a swig of the flask.

'I thought I'd find you in one of the first class cabins,' said Rishaan, surprised.

'Ah! Yes, well. I lost my first class ticket in a poker match last night, so I have to rough it till Athens.' Then as an afterthought, 'Don't tell your mother, though; I don't want any more gossip at Chelmsford.'

'You can tell her yourself if you like. We would like to ask you to dine with us tonight in the restaurant carriage.'

'Really? That would be very considerate, considering my predicament. Tell your mother I would be delighted. But my misfortune at the poker table is our secret, er, what's your name again?'

'Rishaan.'

'Rishaan, it is. My name is Lt. Robert Wordsworth, AFC. Friends call me Buster, because I keep crashing my kites.'

'Spiffing!' said Rishaan. 'See you then!'

'What an eclectic bunch you have traveling with you, Julia,' said Buster at dinner.

'What does eclectic mean?' asked the Princess.

'It means, well, varied, multiple styles, no one form,' said Rishaan's mother.

'I want to be a pilot too,' said Jan. 'Tell me about what's it like.'

'Well, let me see, I was only twenty years old when we flew in Somaliland,' said Buster, decanting the brandy from the bottle on the dinner table into his flask. 'It was the best of times. The de Havilland DH9s are cantankerous old buggers to fly. The engines seize up; they fly like a brick. They were a disaster in the Great War; we couldn't get any height out of them like we could with the DH4s. That means we couldn't go over the enemy fighters. We had to go through them, which isn't very sensible.'

Jan sat wide-eyed at the dinner table; he had hardly touched his food as he listened to every word the lieutenant said. Buster sat back and lit a cigar, cracking a window to let the smoke escape. The Princess was also fascinated by his stories, although she pretended to be slightly bored.

'I was always glad to get up into the air; it was so hot in the desert. Sand everywhere – but up in the sky it's fresh and cool. The air is cleaner, sweeter. We had a great time with Viscount Trenchard. A first-rate chap, a great leader. His favourite trick was to ask the airmen on service, 'What is your number, airman?' Mine was 3074. If the airman had any sense, he would ask the Viscount for his number. '1!' the viscount would counter, much to his delight. He's a great man, the viscount. He was wounded while fighting in South Africa. They say he was an excellent horseman. In any case, he was shot in action and the bullet punctured his lung and dislocated his spine. So he was out of the action and sent home. He could hardly walk, needed sticks to get about. They said it would never get better. Anyway, never a man to give up easily, he went to St. Moritz to get some mountain air. Bored out of his mind he bobsleighed down the Cresta Run and had such a nasty crash at the bottom his spine was dislocated back again into its proper shape and he could walk again!'

'Wow!' said Jan.

'Yes, Hugh—that's the Viscount Trenchard to you children—he told me that story,' said Rishaan's mother.

'Yes, it is a corker,' said Rishaan.

'Hugh and I had a bit of a falling out. We were up in Iraq, fighting the Kurds. The local Iraqis were fed up with the British policies, especially the hard-handed governor, Sir Arnold Wilson, the 'Despot of Mess-Pot.''

'Mess-Pot?' asked Rishaan.

'Yes, Mesopotamia, that's what Iraq used to be called before we changed it. Anyway, the King of the Kurds, Sheik Mahmoud Barzinji, was causing trouble up in the north, so up we went. We bombed a few Kurdish villages. Trenchard told us to use phosphorus bombs and I complained. I was convinced that legally, phosphorus bombs are chemical weapons when used as an anti-personnel weapon. So I said so.'

'What did Hugh say?' asked Rishaan's mother.

'Well, let's put it this way: I was a Group Captain by then. I'm back to being a lieutenant again now.'

'That's unfair!' protested Rishaan.

'Well, it was either that or because of my not marrying Beverly Cheltmine.'

'Yes, well, I think the jury is still out on that one, Lt. Wordsworth,' countered Rishaan's mother.

'Well, I don't mind. I was getting fed up with the responsibility of being a Group Captain anyway. It's much more fun just being a pilot.'

Just then the train entered a tunnel, the increase in air pressure banging the windows, and everything went dark outside. The Princess snuggled up to Rishaan's mother.

'That always frightens me, when the train hits the tunnels,' said Buster, to comfort the Princess. 'But I've learned a trick. The engine driver always blows his whistle just before he enters a tunnel, to warn any people or animals that may walking around inside.'

'I'll tell you another story,' said Buster, taking a swig from his flask. 'This is how I got the name Buster. I was down in South Africa, doing some routine flying—you know the sort of stuff, taking the mail and medicines around. Letting everybody know we, the British, were there. Anyway, the damn engine fails again. It blows a gasket; a piece of engine missed my ear by two inches. Luckily, I had some altitude, so I knew that if I was quick and argus-eyed, I could at least pick the spot I was going to land. Well, unfortunately, I was flying over a jungle, so all I could see was one huge canopy of treetops, no fields or convenient runways.

'Suddenly, I spied a river. It was not ideal, but maybe it was flat and not deep, so I could land. I try my best to manoeuvre, but I'm falling fast; those DH-9s don't glide very well. The DC-9 doesn't have a retractable undercarriage; its wheels always hang down, not like the newfangled crates we have these days. I get it lined up perfectly, but at the last minute, I see the river is not only flowing fast, but it's also rocky and turbulent. I have no choice now, I've committed, and I must land. I hit some boulders, which rip off the wheels and belly flop me on the water. I bang my head on the dashboard, and I'm knocked out for a few seconds.

'I wake up, totally disoriented. To my surprise, I'm floating down the river in my plane. It took me a while to figure it out how I got there, I can tell you. But everything's fine – I'm not seriously hurt; I'm even going in the right direction! The air in the petrol tanks is keeping the plane afloat. Well, I thought, I won't get home as quick as I had hoped, but at least I'm still alive. It's a fast-flowing river and seems to be getting faster and faster, and before I know it, I turn a corner, and there's the largest waterfall I've ever seen in my whole life. And I'm going straight for the edge. There was nothing I could do. I couldn't jump out – the water was too wild. I'd surely drown, and I could never swim against the current to reach the side but would go over the fall anyway. So I had to take my chances. The plane went over the edge, but instead of plummeting down, the wings caught the air, and as if catapulted, it took to flight again, only for a few seconds, simply to glide and land on the shore on the side of the lake at the bottom.'

'Wow,' said Jan.

'And that's why they call me Buster. I'm the only person to crash the same plane twice in the space of a few minutes.'

'I don't believe you!' said the Princess.

'Yes, it's true,' said Rishaan's mother. 'Did they give you a medal, or take one away, because of that?' she asked.

'Nothing, but someone complained that their post was late. There is no pleasing some people.'

'Wow,' said Jan. 'Tell us another!'

'Well, the last one then. This one is for our disbelieving Princess. It was 1925, just finished my time in Somaliland, when we were sent to the Princess's back yard, the country of Waziristan in India. This country is the borderland between India and Afghanistan. It's a difficult terrain, and the tribes that live there are a strong and proud race. We had sent British soldiers in before to stop a rebellion, but it was a pyrrhic victory, with more than a thousand casualties and no conclusive results. So we jumped into our planes and bombed and strafed their mountain strongholds and we were back in time for tea. It only took two months before the rebel leaders asked for an honourable peace. We called it Pink's war, after Wing Commander R.C.M. Pink. It proved to everyone the power of war from the air.

'On one sortie, I had to go and check out one of the valleys of the Maizar River. We didn't know if there were any rebels there so I was just to do some reconnaissance. I followed the river to the west and then flew over a mountain to take a shortcut into the valley on the other side, as the river doubled back on itself. Well, it was a remarkable sight, as I flew over the crest. The whole valley below was swarming with rebels. There must have been more than two thousand of them. They all started shaking their fists at me as I buzzed around above them. Some tried to take pot shots at me, but their old rifles didn't have much range, and as I kept above four hundred feet there was no danger. Some of them threw stones at me, which wasn't very clever, as the stones only fell back down on them. Anyway, it was a strange feeling to be hanging above them, all those angry warriors below, who would gladly tear me limb from limb and drink my blood if they could get their hands on me.

'I teased them a bit, waggling my wings, and blew raspberries. I took some pictures, and then something attracted my attention. There was a group of tents, and next to this encampment were three trees, growing next to each other. Of course, this was too good to be true, so I swung the plane around, lined it up, and over-armed a grenade. It hit the middle tree at the base, blew up, and the tree fell on the tents. I knew some day all that cricket practice would come in handy. They were not pleased down on the ground, so I gave them a hearty wave and buggered off.'

'Wow!' said Jan.

Rishaan loved these stories, but he was very tired. He had been trying to figure out a means of writing in code with Jan, and he was not being successful. Tomorrow they would be in Budapest and he would have to think of something then, before Jan left.

'Thank you, Robert, for a very entertaining evening,' said Rishaan's mother. 'I'm sure the children enjoyed it; it certainly helps make this journey easier for them. However, I think it's time I retired them to their cabins.'

'Thank you, Julia, for letting me dine with you and the children. This was much more agreeable than a few sandwiches in second class. Also, this delicious brandy will help me sleep much more comfortably.'

The next day, Rishaan went looking for Buster again. Maybe he could help with his coding problem. He told Buster he was working on a school project.

'Well, I've never really had to send messages in code,' said Buster, looking a little the worse for the brandy. 'We use code words on the radio, just in case the foe is listening in. I do remember from my classics teacher, Mr. Blightly, the story told by Herodotus. The Greek King Histaiaeus wanted to get his friend Aristagoras to unite with him to attack the Persian King. So he sent him a secret message. He shaved the hair off his messenger and then tattooed the message on his bald head. He waited until the hair grew back, and then sent him to Aristagoras, who shaved the messenger's head to read the letter. If the messenger was intercepted on his way, there were no parchments or wax tablets to seize. Of course, I guess there was also no sense of urgency in those days.'

'I don't think that's a practical option,' said Rishaan.

'Well, there was another example: the Chinese would write their messages on silk, then screw the tissue up into a tight ball, cover it in wax, and swallow it.'

'Again, impractical.'

'Then those are all the options I can think of,' said Buster.

'I've been thinking about the code,' said Rishaan, to Jan, later. 'If we're pen pals we won't be sending each other large documents. So the secret messages we will be sending each other can only be short, maybe only a few sentences. I was thinking that if you spelt a few words wrong in your letter, the words you spell wrong could be the message you wish to send. But I'm frightened it may be too obvious, so write the message backwards: the first word you spell wrong is the last word in the message.'

'I think I can do that,' said Jan, 'but maybe we can figure out a better system at a later date.'

Later that morning the train pulled into Budapest Keleti Train Station. Jan's father arrived to pick up his son. He was grateful to Rishaan's mother for helping, and Jan was very pleased to see his father again. They had a short break before the train would leave again, so Rishaan, Jan and the Princess, accompanied by the Sikh bodyguard and Jan's valet, explored the train station. It was a majestic building, with a large stained glass window frontage and two statues of James Watt and George Stephenson standing in the façade, looking over the square in front.

There was a lot of hustle and bustle, and a lot of soldiers coming from or going to their detachments. There were a lot a people with piles of baggage, as if they had everything they owned with them, and Rishaan wondered if they were refugees. Rishaan also had the uneasy feeling he was being watched. He could not see anybody specific. Once he thought he saw the guard who checked their documents on the train, but it was difficult to see in the crowds. Soon it was time to say goodbye. Rishaan was sorry to see Jan leave. He was not sure what would happen to him, with the changes that were happening in Europe.

'I'll write soon!' shouted Jan, as the train pulled out of the station.

King Zog

THIS IS THE BBC CALLING:

Today, Mussolini's Italy invaded Albania. They faced no significant resistance from the Albanian army, which was ill-equipped to resist. The Albanian army was almost entirely dominated by Italian advisors and officers and was no match for the Italian Army. There was some resistance by small elements in the gendarmerie and general population. King Zog and the rest of the Royal Family have fled into exile.

Rishaan sat with his mother and the Princess in the train cabin reading a book, but he found it hard to concentrate. His mother and the Princess both disliked the cold and had turned up the heating in the carriage. That and the gentle rocking of the train were making Rishaan drowsy, so he decided to go for a walk. He wandered down the carriages, each wagon from a different country in Europe, each with its own style, own character, each with its own story to tell. He began to feel that strange sensation again, as if he was being followed. He didn't dare look back, but he was sure there was someone shadowing him. He began to walk a little faster, but the stranger kept up, matching his pace. Rishaan didn't know what to do. Was this the same person who had arranged for his bag to be stolen in London? Had it to do with the guard who had, unannounced, checked all the passports? Why was he following him? Why didn't he just stop him? He was just a boy, there was nothing he could do. Suddenly, Rishaan heard the train blow its whistle, so he began to run, and as soon as the train hit the tunnel and entered darkness, Rishaan dodged into a cabin and hid behind the door. He could just see a figure, silhouetted, running down the corridor in the direction he had been heading. He quickly doubled back, straight to his mother and the Princess. He decided to stay there for the rest of the journey; he didn't want to take any risks. Anyway, he had promised his father to take care of his mother.

The train had entered the Kingdom of Yugoslavia, passing through Belgrade in Serbia, and then racing on toward the Macedonian border and on into Greece.

'Tell me about Zionism,' said Rishaan to his mother.

'Zionism, yes well, we were talking about it, weren't we?' said Rishaan's mother. 'Zionism is the reason I want to visit Palestine. I want to write about the Jews and the Palestinians. I want to write about the British and why and what they are doing in Palestine. I have told you about the Jews being persecuted through the centuries in their own land, and then again in the countries they had fled to as refugees, or sold to as slaves.

'Palestine itself used to be the homeland of the Philistines, and it is said that they came from the south of Greece, related to the early Mycenaean civilization. They settled on the coastal region around the city of Gaza. They too were plagued by attacks from foreign invaders, and in 604 BC, Nebuchadnezzar II, King of Babylon, exiled the inhabitants of Palestine to Iraq after destroying the Philistine cities. '

'It's confusing,' said Rishaan.

'Even after the twelve tribes of the Israelites came to the area there was instability. If it wasn't the Egyptians who were invading, or Persians invading with their Iraqi army, or Alexander the Great invading with the Greeks, or the Romans invading, it was European Christians invading in the Crusades. If that wasn't enough, there were internal conflicts and civil wars. Finally, the Turks, who had built the Ottoman Empire, invaded in 1516. The Ottoman Empire held the area until the Great War.

'Well, as civilization and enlightenment came, the Jews were treated with respect as individuals, but their culture and traditions were often still forbidden. With this new freedom came the desire to change that, and the only way possible seemed to be that the Jews would have their own country, their own homeland. The first attempt was by an American called Noah, to establish a homeland on Grand Island in the state of New York.'

'So what are the British doing in Palestine?' asked the Princess.

'Well, the Ottomans—that is, the Turks—sided with the Germans during the Great War, so the British sided with the French to take over the area. The British were afraid the Turks would try to take the Suez Canal. This would block ships trying to get to India. Your grandfather played a small part in that; he worked with Lawrence of Arabia, trying to unite all the Arabs against the Turkish Ottomans. Arthur Balfour, our British minister for foreign affairs, laid down plans to establish a Jewish homeland in Palestine. Then in 1917, General Allenby took the British forces into Palestine and invaded the whole Levant right up to Turkey, capturing Jerusalem and defeating the Turks at the Battle of Megiddo.'

'Yes!' said Rishaan. 'I remember the sergeant major telling me about this. General Allenby had sent for Grandfather to tell him how Lawrence of Arabia was doing. The sergeant major had heard that Allenby had taken Jerusalem, so he went from Aqaba to Jerusalem to meet the General. However, Allenby was not there yet; the information was wrong. Grandfather was in luck, though, the Turks had just fled Jerusalem because they were frightened that the British would surround them in a siege. The sergeant major drove up to the gates of the city, only to have the local authorities surrender the city to him. The sergeant major was very pleased with himself; he had achieved single-handedly what Richard the Lionheart had failed to do with the Crusades. General Allenby thought it a great lark.'

'Yes, well, that's your grandfather as usual, getting up to mischief,' said Rishaan's mother. She continued, 'The French got involved with Lebanon and Syria—you'll see that a bit, Rishaan, when we take the ferry to Beirut. They call it the Paris of the East.'

'So the Jews are now returning to Palestine?'

'Many are, not all. Some Jews are even against Zionism. However, the Arabs that live in Palestine are frightened that the Jews that are arriving are taking all the best jobs, buying up all the houses and land. There has been much disquiet about this—assassinations and terrorist attacks. The region is now quiet, but the problem has not been solved. I fear it will not be solved soon.'

'There is so much unrest already in the whole world,' said the Princess.

'Can we invite Buster again tonight? It's the last night,' said Rishaan.

'I don't know,' said the Princess. 'I don't think I like the lieutenant much.'

'Why not?' asked Rishaan.

'Well, he did bomb my country and attack my people,' said the Princess.

'Yes, well, it's not like he meant to,' said Rishaan.

'How could he not mean to?' asked the Princess.

'Well, he, er, he...'

'It was by accident?' asked the Princess.

'No, he was ordered. It wasn't personal. Anyway, he has such ripping yarns!'

'Well, that's ok, then,' said Rishaan's mother. 'You can bomb and destroy as much as you like as long as there's a ripping yarn at the end of it.'

'That's not what I mean,' protested Rishaan.

'All the same, it might be wise to give Buster a miss tonight. Tomorrow we will be in Athens and we have a long journey ahead of us.'

Rishaan wanted to protest, but he remembered that he needed to get the Princess on his side if he was to exchange letters with her, so he changed the conversation.

'I'm still interested in learning Urdu,' he said.

The next day they got off at the Piraeus station, at the harbours near Athens. Princess Anjuli's uncle Prince Mohammed Ali Singh was there to meet them. He still looked slightly worried but was pleased to see his niece. He was staying at the King George II Palace, a majestic hotel in Athens, and had booked rooms for Rishaan and his mother as a thank you for their care of the Princess. Buster Wordsworth said his goodbyes at the railway station. He had to take a ferry to Crete, and then fly a plane to Baghdad.

'I'm to train some rookies, then I'm to fly a Spitfire back to England—all routine stuff,' he said, and then with a wave he disappeared into the steam from the engine that filled the small station.

'It's very kind of you to arrange rooms, Prince Singh,' said Rishaan's mother. 'It will be nice to have a hot bath and sleep in a bed that isn't being shaken about.'

'That I had anticipated,' said the Prince. 'There has been a development. Mahatma Gandhi, the man trying to get India to be independent from the British Raj, has started a hunger strike today. He is protesting the autocratic rule in India.'

'Will there be trouble?' asked Rishaan's mother.

'We hope not, and Gandhi is a man of peace. He will do his utmost to keep the protests non-violent. But we cannot expect one man to keep millions of people in line, especially one sick from fasting. There is no precedent for this; we don't know what is going to happen.'

They spent the next day discovering Athens. Rishaan was glad to be off the train, and the weather was beautiful compared to the cold and foggy London. Rishaan's mother stayed at the hotel and tried to arrange some meetings with contacts in Lebanon and Palestine, but the telegram service was not cooperating. Rishaan and the Princess took the funicular to the top of Mount Lycabettus, accompanied by the Princess's uncle and her bodyguard. There was a magnificent view of the city.

'They say the mountain was made by Athena, who created it when she dropped a mountain she had been carrying from Pallene for the construction of the Acropolis,' said the Princess.

'Do you know a lot about Greek history?' asked Rishaan

'Not really, it was in a tourist pamphlet at the Hotel,' said the Princess, and they both smiled.

The Princess's bodyguard kept a distance, but growled menacingly at everybody, making the local Greeks and tourists nervous.

'So tell me about Singh, your bodyguard,' said Rishaan.

'Sirdar Singh is from the province of Multan, between the left bank of the Indus and the right bank of the Sutlej. In India, his family has been bodyguards for the royal family for centuries. For him it is a matter of honour that I will be safe, as it is my father's wish. He would lay down his life to save mine. He knows that if he dies protecting me, my father will always take care of his family.'

Rishaan thought the Sikh bodyguard was very impressive: tall and physically strong, his incredibly dark eyes shifted around, suspiciously scrutinizing the innocent tourists.

'Sirdar fought against the British in the second Sikh war. It was his job to protect the treasure of the Multan. There was a war, waged by the Diwan Mulraj, who the British had tried to replace as governor of the area. When the British sent a small party of men with the new governor to replace him, the Sikhs revolted, and Goodhar Singh, Sirdar's grandfather, chopped off the head of the British representative with his Talwar sword—the same sword Sirdar has now. This was the start of the revolt.

'The British sent an army to siege the city of Multan. This was a city of 80,000 people. It had many riches, such as chests filled with jewels and copper canisters filled with gold coins. Stacked high were bale upon bale of silks and shawls, and huge stores of wheat and rice. Strong walls with eighty cannons surrounded the city.

'The British brought in their artillery and pounded the walls of the city until two breaches were made. Mortars were fired into the city, and one mortar exploded in the arsenal, setting off the whole of the Mulraj's collection of rocket shells and explosives. More than 800 people were killed and most of the buildings in the centre, including the temples, were destroyed. The shock knocked bottles off tables over two miles away. But the Sikhs were not disheartened, and the survivors defied the British and said that they would fight to the last man.

'The next two days the British pounded the walls and, after more breaches, they tried to storm the city but the Sikhs used everything they could, even stones and broken furniture, to repel the attackers.

'The British managed to get inside the city and a mass slaughter ensued. There was a house-to-house battle, with all the inhabitants being put to the bayonet; no one was to be taken alive. There was a Hindu mosque in the city, defended by Sirdar's grandfather. The British got inside, but it was cramped and they had difficulty fighting with their long muskets with bayonets. There was no room to turn. A corporal fired his musket at Goodhar and missed. In those days it took some time to reload a musket, so the corporal charged Goodhar with his bayonet. Goodhar fought back with his Talwar, but the corporal managed to spear the brave Sikh, and then finished him off by beheading him with his own sword.'

'That's the same sword that beheaded his grandfather?' asked Rishaan.

'Yes. Sirdar doesn't like the British much,' said the Princess.

'Tell him I'm half American.' whispered Rishaan, and the Princess giggled.

'After the defeat of the Sikhs, the famous Koh-i-Noor diamond was taken and given to Queen Victoria, and the boy Maharajah, Duleep Singh, was made to sign his kingdom away. Sirdar's father, Kuldip Singh, was the boy Maharajah's bodyguard and accompanied him to his exile in England. The Maharajah, when he grew up, made Sirdar's father swear that someday the Koh-i-Noor diamond would return to the Punjab. Sirdar, too, has sworn that if ever he gets the chance, he will get the diamond back.'

'Where is the diamond now?' asked Rishaan.

'It's in the Tower of London. It's part of the King's crown jewels. We went to see it once. Sirdar was grumpy the rest of the day.'

'How could you tell?' asked Rishaan, and they laughed.

It was time to go. Suddenly, the Princess held Rishaan's hand. 'Do promise to write to me,' she said, and looked into his eyes. 'I do miss London so much, even in the wintertime. Write to me and tell me everything that is going on.'

'I promise,' said Rishaan, 'and you must tell me everything about what's happening in the Punjab. And when everything's back to normal I will come and visit, if Sirdar will let me.'

The Princess smiled, but she looked sad.

After he left, Rishaan felt sadness as well. He liked the Princess, and he would miss her.

The next day, Rishaan and his mother took the ferry from Athens to Beirut. It was a night crossing, on a calm Mediterranean. When they arrived the next day, they stayed at the Palm Beach Hotel in Beirut, with a beautiful view over the Mediterranean Sea and Mount Lebanon. Rishaan could see how happy his mother was, arranging meetings, contacting friends, writing a journal and doing research—she was totally in her element. Rishaan promised her he would take photographs for her articles and he walked the streets of Beirut taking some shots with his Leica. He bought a present from a street peddler, a pendant for his mother. He would give it to her when they were back in London as a thank-you for the trip.

They spent a few days in the old French colonial city, then they hired a jeep and drove down the coast to Palestine. They were without servants now, who had stayed in Beirut until called by Julia. Rishaan's mother wore a hijab, a head scarf, worn by most women in Palestine, but also wore a white shirt and trousers, which was very western.

'You're looking very eclectic, Mother,' said Rishaan, and she laughed.

The weather was beautiful, and Rishaan taught his mother Arabic words as the old coast road twisted between the olive trees.

Rena Achildiev held tightly to her grandmother. Ever since they had left Russia, she had been afraid of the new experiences, sights and sounds she had encountered. Her father had said they were going to the land of milk and honey, but this was so strange to her. Since she had been born six years ago she had only known her village and her family. Now, her parents had decided to move to Palestine, or as they called it, Israel.

'We Bukharian Jews have to go back to the homeland,' her father would say at the dinner table. Rena did not understand. Samarkand in Russia was her homeland—that was where she was born, that was where her father was born, and his father.

That was where her friends were. How could she go back to somewhere she had never been to?

'It is not safe here for us Jews. The Soviets are taking our lands, and soon there will be war with Germany. I'm sure of it, and they hate Jews as well. We must stick together; we must have our own country to defend ourselves. Now we're too divided,' her father explained. Her grandmother did not want to go either, but she had seen the rise of anti-Semitism and feared the consequences if they stayed.

'Don't worry, my little Rena,' she said, 'you have lived in Samarkand for only six years; I have lived there for nearly sixty. We will get through this together.'

When they reached the border of Palestine they were put on a bus that had bars and chicken wire on the windows. She did not know why; the whole country was strange. It was hot and dry, and the terrain was brown and yellow and stony, not green like the hills back home.

'We're going to a beautiful city,' her grandmother told her. 'It's called Jerusalem, and we will be staying with friends in the Sh'hunat Buhori. They call it the Bukharian quarter, so we will not be alone. Maybe we will meet someone we know.'

The bus was hot as it trundled along the provincial road, although a breeze came into the bus, as most of the windows were broken. Rena wanted some water but didn't dare ask. She could see how freighted everybody was. Rena's father looked confused.

'Are you looking for the land of milk and honey?' laughed the bus driver. 'The Palestinians let their goats eat all the grass, then the soil dried and blew away into the desert!'

Mohammad Ha'am's eldest brother was in a rage. Mohammad's brother had tried to buy a farm so that he could move out of his parent's house. Only then could he marry the love of his life, Fatima. All he wanted was to start a family and be a good Palestinian. He had saved every Palestinian pound and mil coin he could earn. But before he could scrape enough money together, a group of Jews had bought the land he was hoping to get so they could turn it into a kibbutz. His uncle had promised to help him, but his wife and children were killed in a raid on his village of Atteel, and even though that was more than a year ago, his uncle was too distraught to be capable of helping anyone.

Mohammad hated it when his older brother was angry. He just wanted to play games, be happy, and tend the goats. He loved the stories his brothers told him about how they had tried to fight the Turks, and his father's stories about when he went to Jerusalem. His father had even been to Mecca to participate in the hajj. Mohammad's father had been a wealthy man in the village, but the Turks had stolen all his livestock and destroyed his crops when they retreated from the British. Since then he had been working hard to build up a livelihood, but it was getting harder and harder.

'Look!' shouted Mohammad's brother, 'There are more Jews!'

Mohammed looked, and down the road from his village, he could see a bus trundling toward them. His brothers picked up some stones, and as the bus got nearer, they threw the stones at the bus. The stones just bounced off the side of the bus and the chicken wire, but the passengers inside screamed. Mohammed picked up a small stone and placed it in his shepherd's sling.

He was not good with the sling, but he had been practicing. He swirled the sling a few times around his head, then let go of one of the cords, and the stone shot off toward the bus. The stone was small enough to pass through the chicken wire and hit the driver on the temple, who swerved to the right, and then there was a loud bang on the other side of the bus. The driver managed to keep control of the bus, but kept his foot down, as he did not want the boys outside to surround them. They might have other weapons.

'Stop! Stop the bus!' shouted Rena's father.

They had been driving for a few hours, and Rishaan's mother was getting tired. She wanted to be in Jerusalem before nightfall. There was an old slow bus in front of them that was blocking the road. After a while, they approached a village with a small square, and Rishaan's mother thought that would be a good place to pass. Just as they reached the square, they tried to overtake the bus, but the bus suddenly started speeding up. Rishaan's mother accelerated more to try and get ahead of the bus. Suddenly, the bus swerved to the right, blocking the road entirely. Rishaan's mother stamped on the brake, but nothing happened, then she veered off the road to miss the bus, and the jeep rolled down an embankment. It was the last thing Rishaan remembered.

He awoke, lying in a shallow stream, the water cold, his arm hurting, the water glittering in the afternoon sun. He could hear people shouting in the distance. He didn't understand. Where was he? He tried to move, but a charge of excruciating pain shot down his arm, and he lost consciousness again.

He opened his eyes. Now he was on dry land, but he was wet and cold. His head was resting on a shepherd's jacket. He was surrounded by people. Some of them were Palestinians; some of them were orthodox Jews. They stood there, looking at him.

'Are you all right?' asked one, in Arabic.

'Yes,' said Rishaan. 'No,' he added. Again he tried to move, and again the intense pain and the loss of consciousness.

There was a blur of movement, shapes and colours. He heard voices, whispering. He felt himself being moved, but he had no energy to protest. He drifted from one dream to another; the voices went away and then there were more whispers. He knew he had to get out of his dream state but somehow they would not let him. He dreamed that he had to crack a code first before he could leave his dream, but he felt too drowsy to think properly. He saw pieces of a shape; he tried to piece them together, but they would not fit, and the shapes kept changing. His arm hurt. Finally, the pieces began to fall together, and slowly the shapes turned into a form, a white room. There was man sitting next to his bed, reading a book. It was his father.

'Hello Father,' said Rishaan.

His father looked at Rishaan and put the book down. 'Good to see you're back,' his father whispered. His father looked very pale and tired.

Rishaan tried to sit up, but his arm hurt again.

'Try to keep still,' said his father. 'You have broken your arm, and you have to keep it still while it sets properly.'

'How's Mother doing?' asked Rishaan. 'Has she done something to her arm, as well?'

'I'm afraid your mother has had a much more serious accident,' his father said.

Rishaan could see that his father was upset. His father did not seem to be able to say anything more; he seemed beside himself with grief. Rishaan had never seen his father like this; he knew that something had changed forever.

'Tell me, Father,' said Rishaan, 'are we still a fortunate family?'

Before the Storm

THIS IS THE BBC CALLING:

It has been rumoured that the German and Soviet governments are secretly beginning an agreement with the aim of dividing up Eastern Europe between them. Some German politicians have informed the British government of German economic problems, which they state threaten the survival of the Nazi regime. They advise that if a stand is made to defend Poland, then Hitler would not be able to go to war.

It has also been reported that Sweden, Norway, and Finland are refusing Germany's offer of non-aggression pacts.

Further, the British government has issued a directive sharply restricting Jewish immigration to Palestine.

Rishaan had been back in London for a month now, and it had been the most miserable month of his life. It had passed in a blur, Rishaan feeling exhausted and overwhelmed by a sense of apathy he had never experienced before. There had been a memorial service for his mother. A great many people had attended: the Prime Minister, Churchill, the American ambassador, many friends from the press. Grandfather had turned up for the service, despite his fear of the outside world and Zulus, though he needed the help of a great deal of whiskey and spent most of the service supporting one of the church columns. There was even a movie star hanging onto Robert Capa's arm. Capa gave Rishaan a small Leica camera; his had been lost in Palestine. Rishaan still had the rolls of film that he had taken, but he didn't want to develop them; he couldn't face seeing his mother in the pictures.

It had all passed in a haze. Rishaan's father was too distraught to do much and had received leave from his work. They planned to go back to America for a long vacation, staying with Rishaan's father's family in New Hampshire. Rishaan was glad to be getting away from London; it was raining outside, cold and miserable.

Rishaan thought it might be a good idea to go, and they were taking a trans-Atlantic liner to get there. Normally that would be fun, but nothing he could think of would be fun without his mother. Just thinking of sailing on the ship reminded him of the times they had done that together as a family.

A few days later Rishaan lay in the sergeant major's tent in the sergeant major's living room; it seemed a safe place for him to be. His arm was in a sling, and it still hurt. Rishaan's grandfather looked out of the window at the wretched weather. Rishaan had heard about people being depressed. He thought it meant just being very sad. Now he knew what those people were feeling. It was the worst feeling in the world. He would rather be sick, break a leg, and break his arm a thousand times over. He felt as if there was no meaning to anything, no sense of anything having any purpose. Everything was a waste of time. He wanted to feel different. Angry, neutral, indifferent.

Anything but this.

Rishaan listened to the water slowly cooking on the gas burner. He held the pendant in his hand that he had bought for his mother. It comforted him. He had been visiting the sergeant major every day since he had returned to London. The sergeant major didn't try to comfort him; the sergeant major knew from experience that it would take time, so he just let

Rishaan visit, and sometimes they would sit for hours without saying anything. Rishaan figured that the sergeant major had his own grieving to do.

'I was your age as well, when it happened,' said the sergeant major, as if from nowhere.

'What, Grandfather?' asked Rishaan.

'I was a bugle boy with the British Infantry. Twelve years old, I was. I had been recruited into the Army because I was an orphan, living on the streets of Liverpool. The army had taken me in. Cared for me and fed me. I was as proud as a twelve-year-old boy could be. I was soon serving under Lord Chelmsford in Africa. You could not imagine how excited I was to be going on an adventure to a land so far away. When we got there things started to change. I lost some friends to disease. The mercenaries we hired were tough, rough men. Still, for a poor boy from Liverpool, it was amazing—the colours and smells of Africa.

'We camped at a place called Isandlwana. It was a rugged place, Zulu country, with a few trees, long dry grass and rocky outcrops. It was as hot as bugger out there. I had never known anything like it. There were about 1300 of us, about 500 British soldiers and the rest mercenaries and locals. A rough lot they were, not to be trusted. Kill ye for a shilling, they would. We put the wagons in a circle to make a defensive camp but we didn't dig in because word was that if there were any Zulus in the area they would only be about 500 or so. I guess we were kind of cocky about it. It was going to be a long day. I was up early, to blow the bugle. When I had done that, I had some breakfast. Before my other duties would start, I walked off into the bush to do my ablutions.

'The sun was just rising over the ridge. It was stunning, pouring orange over the crests and ridges, the gold pouring down as the sun rose higher. It lit up the dark blue sky with orange streaks, reflecting off the underside of the high altitude clouds. It was going to be a beautiful day. I just walked and walked. It was so peaceful out there. It was good to get away from the noise and bustle of all those rough adults. It was so good to be on my own. It was serene, and the grassy terrain reminded me of England. I let the tall grass brush against my hands as I walked. I must have been daydreaming, as I walked for a long time, watching the clouds, the exotic birds, and the sunrise over the ridge.

'Then a twig snap woke me from my dreaming. The long grass in front of me had elongated stalks sticking out that had blades on the end. They looked like spears, and weird flowers that looked like muskets. At first, I wasn't sure, but then I could see a face hiding in the long grass. Slowly the man stood up. It was a Zulu warrior. He was a big man, with sinewy muscles and a fierce painted face. I knew immediately I was in very serious trouble. Then another Zulu warrior stood up, and another. Then a whole wave of warriors appeared out of the grass. Twelve thousand warriors, standing in total silence. I could see that they were wearing war-paint. They looked magnificent and terrifying. Time stood still for a second, but I knew that this was it; my short life was over. I could not be saved; I was too far from the camp. I could never outrun these athletic warriors.

'They were out to make battle with the invading colonial British, and I was an enemy soldier who could give away their position and the precious element of surprise. I knew that they never take prisoners. I just stood there, the water bottle I was holding slipped out my hand and fell to the ground. I looked at them, and for an instant, they all just looked at me. Then an amazing thing happened. The fright I had disappeared and I became very calm, almost serene. I accepted that there was nothing I could do about my predicament; it was just a question of me accepting the coup de grâce - the death blow. There was a silence, nobody moved. The first warrior looked around, then picked up his machete and walked over to me. I just stood there, in peace, ready for the inevitable. He raised the knife to strike, and I closed my eyes, not even hoping that it would be quick, just accepting, unquestioning. I tried to keep still; I didn't want him to misjudge the blow, to just wound me and then leave me to die a slow death.

'There was a pause. It seemed like a long time and I wondered if I was dead. I opened my eyes. The warrior was still holding his machete up, a silhouette against the morning sun, but he just looked down at me. Maybe it was because I was only a boy, and that I was just standing there with my eyes closed that had confused him. He hesitated. One of his comrades hissed angrily at him; it sounded like 'kill him'. The warrior turned to the other warrior and whispered angrily back. Then he turned round again and slashed down with all his might.

'But I was gone. Sense had poured back into me and I ran like the wind. He ran after me; in fact, the remaining 12,000 warriors ran after me as well, like a silent swarm of bees, for they knew, that once I was back at the camp the element of surprise was gone. The attack was on. The warriors were close behind. I could hear their feet hitting the sand as they ran. The warrior with the machete gained ground quickly on me. I knew I was too far away from the camp to reach it. His strong, athletic legs brought him closer to me with every stride.

'I knew I was doomed; there was nothing or nobody who could save me now. I was at peace; I knew that this was my time. A serene feeling swept again through me, tranquil, accepting. I was to be the first kill of a day of killing, but I was determined he would have to work for it. I refused to be an easy prey. The warrior behind me swiped at me with his machete and missed then, unbalanced, he fell over, but he was promptly replaced by another warrior. The chase continued, and I managed to reach the corner that would be bringing me in full view of the encampment. I had my bugle with me, so I brought it to my lips. Maybe my last deed would be to warn my friends and save some lives. But I was so out of breath all that came out was a few pathetic belching noises.

'The warriors just behind me seemed to hesitate; they knew that once they were in view of the camp their attack was on, it had not been started on their terms, but the mass of warriors were now in full flight and they continued their chase, colliding into the warriors who had hesitated. I ran and ran, puffing in vain on the bugle, and then to my amazement, the soldiers at the British camp started shooting at me. With Martini-Henry rifles and Gatling guns. Not only were 12,000 Zulu warriors chasing me from behind, I was running toward a 1500-strong firing squad. Bullets parted my hair and clipped my ears. The bugle was shot clean out of my hand. Sand spat into the air as the bullets hit the ground. Zulus around me fell to the ground.

'Then the Zulus, now into full war charge, started to overtake me. After what had been almost complete silence, the Zulus took up a war cry that was practically deafening. Their goals now set on the encampment, instead of running in front of the Zulus I was now running with and among the Zulus. Soon I was not only running but also jumping over the bodies that lay in front of me. We crashed into the camp like a tidal wave, rocking the wagons on their axles, and almost knocking them over. The thick thud of the warriors hitting into wooden wagons filled the air. I squirted underneath a wagon and as I came out the other side a startled British soldier almost bayoneted me, before a Zulu warrior too knocked him to the ground. I picked myself up and ran to the other side of the encampment, under the wagons and out the other side. I ran up over the rocky Isandlwana feature, down the other side, across the plain, across the Buffalo River and halfway to Pietermaritzburg. They found me two days later, hiding up a tree.

'The soldiers and civilians back at the camp were massacred. Only 50 escaped. The bodies of the dead were ripped open in a Zulu ritual to free the spirit of the dead and to stop the body swelling up. The cadavers were stabbed many times in the 'washing of the spears', where every warrior was obligated to have stabbed an enemy, even after death.

'I was one of the few survivors. They questioned me afterward, but the shock had been so great I couldn't speak. I couldn't say a word. The doctor called it 'soldier's heart' or 'nostalgia'. I can remember still being in that detachment, that serenity. I was detached; it was as if I stayed in that tree for a year, looking down on life around me. I felt disconnected from the real world.

'There was another reason why I didn't talk. I blamed myself for the massacre. If I hadn't gone off for a walk on my own, but stayed at the camp like I was told to, maybe the Zulus would not have attacked. I felt it was me who had started the whole thing. I should be dead like the rest of the soldiers and civilians. They had been my family; they had trusted me. Finally a fellow bugler befriended me, and after he won my confidence, I told him what had happened. He told the sergeant, who took me to one side.

'Now listen here, bugler,' he said. 'There's no need to blame ye'self. The Zulus were waiting for the British army to decamp and make their way up country. If they had attacked when the army was on the move then they would have been exposed and nobody would have survived the massacre. Because they could defend themselves in a camp, the Zulus suffered a great loss, so much so they could never again get together such a great force. In addition, the politicians in London could not leave such a defeat unpunished, and so were forced to send more men and munitions to finish the job. Which they should have done in the first place. So if you ask me, bugle boy, it was you who saved the day.'

'It was a nice thing for him to say, and they even gave me a medal, which the sergeant made himself. After that I did not stop talking for a month. But the nightmares never left. It was always the same, always the Zulus.'

Rishaan's grandfather smiled at Rishaan, then looked out at the rain for a while. 'Never blame yourself Rishaan,' he said. 'There's nothing you can do about this accidental life we live.'

After tea, Rishaan went upstairs to look around. After Palestine, the shabby rooms filled with boxes did not scare him much anymore. He saw a large photo album lying next to one of the boxes; he had not seen it before. He guessed that the sergeant major had found it recently and had been looking at it. Rishaan opened it up; there were many black and white photographs of Rishaan's grandfather's parents on the first few pages, three pages of the sergeant major's wedding, then lots of photographs of Rishaan's mother, first as a baby, then later growing up. Rishaan did not want to look at the pictures—he was sad enough as it was—but he could not help himself.

Suddenly, the spell was broken by a familiar sound. It was the telephone, upstairs in the attic. Rishaan hesitated. He did not want to go up; he had had enough adventure for a lifetime. He was now also worried about his father. His father had stopped smoking his pipe and was now chain-smoking cigarettes. Without his wife, and now temporarily without his work, he was glum and depressed. He knew that his father did not blame him for the accident, but he did not want to run the risk of disappointing him in any way.

Rishaan did not want to cause trouble; he did not want his father to worry about him. Nevertheless, the telephone continued to ring; Rishaan just stared at the staircase that led up to the attic.

The telephone continued to ring, mesmerizing, beckoning Rishaan to come and answer. Finally, after what seemed like an eternity, it stopped. Rishaan felt disappointed. For a few precious moments, his mind had been taken off his mother, away from the melancholy he was feeling. He regretted not answering the telephone. Maybe it was something important, something he could do to save lives, help to get Europe out of the mess it was in, maybe even help some of the persecuted Jews.

The telephone suddenly started ringing again, and Rishaan was up the stairs as if he was being chased by Zulus. He swung open the trap door and ran to the phone.

'Hello?' he gasped.

'There will be two new packages,' said the woman. 'The first package is for decoding. Please return it as quickly as possible. The second package is for you to deliver. It is a small package. Please do not lose it. They will be delivered tomorrow.' And with that she hung up.

That's strange, thought Rishaan. He wondered what it could be. He decided not to tell the sergeant major. He wanted to keep his options open about whether he would do what they were asking. He had caused enough trouble, and his father was in no mood for more.

When he arrived home there was another letter waiting for him. It was from Jan Jágr. It had been opened by the Polish customs and maybe by the Germans as it had travelled to Britain, but the message was still readable.

Dear Rishaan

As agreed on our train journey with the Orient Express I am sending you this letter. Now I am in Poland. I am staying at a beautiful house on a hil. It is looking down on the city and is next to a curch. As you know, Hitler has declared my country a protectorate of Germany. My country, Czechoslovakia, has ceased to exist. My father thought it safer for me to travel to Poland and stay with some family. My grandmother is Jewish; we do not know if the Germans will make this a problem for her or even for us. Everything is unsure. It was dangerous leaving the country. There were lots of refugees. Many left the country illegally. They tel that they will be safe in Poland, as Poland has signed treaties with Frans und Britan who have promised to come to shou their help if Germany invades. I was in the last carriage of the last train that left Czechoslovakia. I saw the borders close behind me, and my country disappear into the dark. I hope that one day I wil see it again, but it will not be for a long time, I'm afraid. I arrived in Warsaw the next day just as the sun had kracked the skyline. I think that I will like Poland, but the Polish language is for me still a bit of an enigme.

Anyway, hope to see you soon...

Jan!

Rishaan wrote out the words that had been spelt wrong.

Hil curch tel Frans und Britain shou wil kracked enigme.

It didn't make much sense, but then Rishaan remembered he had asked Jan to write his message backwards. He corrected the spelling and re-wrote it back to front.

Enigma cracked will show France and Britain tell Church Hill.

This seemed very interesting. Rishaan did not know what it meant, but maybe Churchill did.

The next day Rishaan visited the sergeant major, and as the woman on the telephone had promised, there was a package waiting for him. Rishaan pretended it was not important, that it was just something he had to take to America with him as a promise to his father. Rishaan's grandfather did not ask any more questions; he just told Rishaan to take care.

'Is it OK if I look at your souvenirs?' he asked.

'Yes, you may use the telephone,' replied the sergeant major. Rishaan grinned; his grandfather was not as crazy as he made out to be.

Rishaan ran up the stairs to the attic. He picked up the telephone, he heard a buzzing sound on the other side, with some static, and then someone picked up the receiver on the other end.

'Yes?' said the woman.

'I have a message for Churchill,' said Rishaan. 'Tell Churchill that Enigma has been cracked by the Polish secret service, and they want to show it to the British and French.'

There was a silence on the other end, and then she replied, 'Yes, I'll give Mr. Churchill your message' and she hung up. It seemed to have made an impression on her.

When Rishaan went downstairs, he found his friend and bodyguard Sam waiting for him. Rishaan was pleased to see him.

'Are we up to our old tricks again, me old China plate?' asked Sam.

'Earning another sixpence, are we?' asked Rishaan.

They got to Brian's house, after taking several detours without any problem, although they had the suspicion that someone was following them. Brian was in the middle of one of his projects.

'Aha, gentleman, you arrive at a most fortuitous time. I need someone to try out my newest invention.' Brian picked up something that looked like a suitcase. It had several dials and lamps on it and a small antenna.

'What is it?' asked Sam.

'I call it a 'distance control'. You can use it to turn the radio on or off, and it can even change stations, while sitting comfortably in your chair. It has no wires. Try it.'

Sam sat down in a chair and Brian handed him his distance control.

'Blimey, it's heavy,' he said.

'Just turn it on, then with these switches you can turn the radio on, and change stations. I want to see if you can figure out how it works. I call it a test of usability.'

Sam fiddled around for a while, without much success, until he got an electric shock and the apparatus gave off a puff of smoke.

'Blimey – are you trying to kill me?' said Sam, pushing the device off his lap onto the ground, breaking it.

'Oh dear, back to the drawing board,' sighed Brian.

'What would be the use of it?' asked Rishaan.

'Well I was thinking it might be useful for old people and pregnant women. I doubt if an able-bodied man would want to be seen using one. I'm hoping the technology I've created would then be applied to another invention of mine, the transportable telephone. A telephone without a wire with which one can roam the streets, deep in conversation,' said Brian.

'Why would anyone want one of those? Sounds dangerous; besides, there are telephone boxes everywhere,' said Rishaan.

'It would be useful for policemen and pregnant women,' concluded Brian.

'If I had a bun in the oven I wouldn't want one of them things on my lap,' declared Sam.

'Yes, well, it's still all experimental. Tell me, Rishaan, have you brought us yet another riddle to ponder?'

Rishaan placed a package on the table. It was a large envelope containing coded documents.

Rishaan felt sad about leaving his friends. He wanted to work on deciphering the document as well, but he knew that a break would do him good, and he had to take care of his father.

That night they had a special guest to dinner. It was King Zog, the exiled king of Albania. He was a friend of the family, and they had been introduced at the Ambassadors Ball in Paris a few years before.

Zog was a self-made king. He had risen from governor of a province in Albania to prime minister, president and had crowned himself king of the newly unified Albania. All the other kings that Rishaan knew were born into position. He liked it that King Zog had made himself king. Another thing Rishaan liked about King Zog was that he had survived 55 assassination attempts. King Zog told him this was due to two things.

'First, in Albania, it is very common to have a blood vengeance about something. For example, I had broken off an engagement just before I became king. She would have been a great wife but a lousy queen,' he explained. However, her father was obliged by Albanian tradition to kill him. 'Maybe he did try, I don't know, it might have been one of the attempts.'

'Secondly,' he went on, 'Albanians are not very good assassins,' and he would laugh out loud which often led to him having a coughing fit. Rishaan's father explained to him that Zog always had a bodyguard with him and carried a gun. He had once been attacked while visiting the Opera in Vienna and had drawn his pistol and fought back. King Zog was the only head of state ever to have exchanged fire with his potential assassins.

King Zog had now arrived in London from Paris and was lobbying the British Government. Tonight he was visiting to discuss how America could help him and his people. The American ambassador had not wanted to meet with King Zog yet, so he had delegated the meeting to Rishaan's father. King Zog was not happy about what he saw as a slight from the Americans, but swallowed his pride. Rishaan's father felt it best to keep the meeting business-like and about what King Zog wanted from America. He also kept Rishaan out of the room, because he knew King Zog smoked constantly.

The door to the dining room was open, so Rishaan watched from the staircase. He could not hear what they were saying, but King Zog was very passionate and he raised his voice several times. He looked frustrated when he left in a storm of cigarette smoke and what seemed like swearing in Albanian.

Rishaan saw his father watch King Zog leave, and he remained there for a while after he had gone. His father looked sad. No matter what he personally felt, it was his job to follow the American foreign policy. There was nothing he could do.

A week later they went to Southampton and took the Cunard liner Aquitania for the trip to New York. The journey was uneventful, even boring, and Rishaan and his father settled in for a five-day voyage.

Rishaan had noticed that his father did not want to talk about Julia. He changed the subject, or avoided the whole issue altogether. Rishaan was sure it was just too painful for him to talk about. However, as the journey established its routine,

Rishaan needed to talk about the trips they had made together. His father did not cut him off, but was not really participating either. Rishaan knew he had to remember his mother, to put her in his verbal memories. To tell the stories he had of her so they would become more fixed in his memories. On the third night, after dinner as they played poker together in the cabin, Rishaan felt he had to talk more about his mother. He had accepted that his father might not want to join in, but his father was not discouraging him either. It just felt good to talk about her; it brought her back to life, if only in fleeting moments.

Slowly his father joined in, and they remembered the great moments they had together. This helped Rishaan a lot, and he felt it helped his father as well. Rishaan finally felt that a tension between them had broken; they no longer needed to filter and edit everything they said to each other. They could be themselves again.

They stayed with friends in New York, and then caught a train out west, to Denver, then to his to visit Rishaan's father's ranch.

Rishaan loved staying at his grandfather's ranch. It was more a hobby for his grandfather than a source of income, although he made it clear it was no frivolity, it made a profit. Rishaan and his parents called him the Captain, because he had made his fortune, or as he always said, his FIRST fortune, as a 'captain of industry'. Richard had a sergeant major for one grandparent and a Captain for another. The Captain was a big man, with large hands and a tough weather-beaten face. He was more at home on his ranch herding cattle or riding across the

Bryce canyon than he was wearing a suit and working in the city. He always wore his Stetson hat.

Rishaan remembered being at a dinner party and there were a group of industrialists enjoying brandy and cigars discussing wealth. The Captain was then visiting his son in England and he was, as usual, loudly entertaining the guests.

'Well, as a wealthy man and amateur biologist, I found it my duty to classify the affluent species into a main group with sub-species. You have the main species, Homo Prosperous.

'This can be divided into two main sub-species – Homo Richus Senilus and Homo Richus Nova. Locally known as Old and New Money. Old Money is an endangered species and is at this moment protected by the government, but the future looks bleak. This is due to its conservative attitude and lack of adaptation to changing environments. They feed all over the world but their breeding grounds are found mostly in Europe. New Money is thriving, finding strength in change and exploiting new opportunities. They too are found all over the world but America is their natural habitat.'

This made the gentleman laugh, but Rishaan found it very interesting.

'Can you classify the poor, Grandfather?' he asked.

'I'm afraid not,' said the Captain. 'I'm afraid it's one size fits all.'

'I beg to disagree,' said an old man, puffing on a cigar, whom Rishaan suspected of being old rich. 'Some are born into poverty; others have poverty thrust upon them.'

Rishaan liked it when the old men laughed. It was deep and hearty, even if he didn't know why they laughed.

His grandfather kept horses and steer and looked after his grandniece Shelly, who Rishaan was afraid of. His grandfather said that she was more trouble than all the other animals put together. But Rishaan knew he meant that she was fun trouble, because he doted on her. She was loud and energetic, with big red hair. She would whoop and shout her way through the day. Rishaan had heard rumours that Shelly stayed at the ranch because she got up to too much misfortune living in urban New York. She could get up to trouble in Monument Valley without causing too much damage. His grandfather once said that before Shelly came to Monument Valley it used to be a forest, but Rishaan guessed he was joking.

It was 6 o'clock in the morning when Shelly burst into Rishaan's room in full cowgirl regalia, jumped up and down on his bed shouting, 'Get up! Get up! It's time to go horse riding!' in a fake British accent, then ran out again. Rishaan swore that if she had guns with her, and sometimes she did, there would now be holes in the ceiling.

Rishaan went to the main house and had a hearty breakfast while Shelly ran around outside chasing the chickens and the dogs. When he was finished his grandfather pushed him outside to go play with her. She loved the ranch but missed company, especially someone her own age.

'Here's your gear; get it on, and we can saddle up!' she said.

Rishaan had ridden horses before, on his grandfather's ranch, but it was on trails with his mother and father and was scenic and restrained. He knew he was in trouble with Shelly.

He put his gear on and climbed onto the horse with some difficulty. Shelly jumped on to her horse and yelled 'Yii-haa!' She slapped Rishaan's horse on its butt, and off they went.

'Bring him back in one piece!' shouted his grandfather, who looked worried.

They galloped for some way into the Valley; the huge sandstone buttes glowed orange in the dawn sun. Rishaan could not believe it was still only 7 o'clock – he felt as if he had a full day behind him already. The horses slowed down and they relaxed. Shelly started telling him all about Colorado and Arizona and the snakes and scorpions she had caught.

'Let's try some gun practice – can you shoot?' asked Shelly.

'Of course I can shoot!' said Rishaan. He had shot some guns before when visiting his grandfather, and his father had taught him when they lived in the Sudan. However, he did not have much experience and feared the combination of Shelly and firearms. He did not want to seem like a wimp, that a girl could out-shoot him, even though it was Shelly.

'Grandfather insists I always have a firearm with me when I go out. He says I can kill snakes and wild things, and protect myself. I can even call for help – if I shoot three times in a row then he will come and get me. Of course, they can't hear us from here, but if I fall and break my leg then when I see someone I can shoot my gun. Grandfather told me to try not to shoot the person who's trying to rescue me.'

'Sounds smart to me,' said Rishaan.

They dismounted, and Shelly placed some stones on a boulder. She loaded her rifle and aimed at the rocks. With the first shot she blasted the stones in different directions. The single rifle shot sounded out into the vastness of the valley.

'Good shot!' praised Rishaan.

'Your turn!' she shouted, hardly containing her excitement.

It was still early in the morning but it was already getting hot. He hoped they would not be out in the sun all day; there was no shade anywhere. Rishaan set up some more stones on the rock then aimed the rifle. It was a heavy gun, the heaviest he had ever used, and he had to use all his strength to keep the muzzle pointed in the right direction. He pulled the trigger, and the recoil from it knocked him flat on his back. Shelly burst out in laughter and did a dance.

'Again!' she shouted.

They tried some more target practice, and Rishaan got more control over the gun. With his last shot he sent the stones spinning.

'We are running out of ammo, let's stop now,' he said.

Shelly grabbed the gun and removed the ammo. He saw that, despite all her bravado, she was sensible when it came to things that were dangerous. She looked comfortable and professional with the firearm, treating it properly. He remembered she had broken her arm once with a fall from her horse. She never complained once about it, and when it was in plaster carried like a trophy. He had respect for her, even admiration.

'Okay – let's have a race back to the ranch!' she said. 'First one round the Devil's finger,' she said, pointing at the large sandstone butte, 'and back to the ranch, wins!'

'Okay,' said Rishaan and he walked over to the horse.

'No, not like that, come here,' she said, and she pulled him over to a spot a few hundred feet from the horses. 'On a count of three, we run to the horses, ready?'

'Okay,' he said.

'2 – 3!' she shouted and ran, leaving Rishaan behind. Soon, he was eating her dust as she sprang on the horse and headed off. Rishaan ran after her, but in his attempt to jump on his horse, miscalculated and fell over the other side, landing on the ground. The horse was not impressed and started walking off. Rishaan started chasing after it, which irritated the horse even more and it started trotting away from Rishaan.

After trying to catch his horse for ten minutes, he finally got onto the horse. However, the horse now knew who was boss and responded poorly to his commands. The horse soon got bored, and started wandering back to the ranch with Rishaan on his back.

Rishaan got back to the ranch just as Shelly galloped in behind.

'I won!' said Rishaan, and Shelly just stared at him in disbelief.

'You ate my dust! I won fair and square!' protested Shelly, but Rishaan just laughed.

'I guess,' he said.

That night his father was agitated. There had been bad news on the radio. Germany was threatening Poland. Everybody was down, and seemed exhausted. Nobody wanted another war with Germany, not after the horrors of the First World War. That was supposed to be the war to end all wars.

After he had gone to bed, he heard his father talking to his grandfather in the library. His father seemed concerned, so Rishaan sneaked down. He could see the silhouettes of his father and grandfather against the roaring fire. They sipped brandies, and Grandfather smoked his cigar while his father smoked his pipe. The room was filling up with smoke.

'I am so concerned about what's happening in Europe,' said his father. 'The markets are concerned too; it's bad for business, and it's bad for everybody.'

His grandfather added, 'But it's not your concern. You have just had something tragic happen to you. You need to rest. Reevaluate. Rishaan needs you.'

'Everything that happens, every bit of news, every political statement—it makes me think of what Julia would think of that, what would Julia do? It's not fair, there are so many people in this world who do nothing with their lives, and Julia did so much, and had so much to do.'

He stared into the fire for a while. Rishaan's grandfather knew this was a time not to advise, but to listen.

'I miss her. I miss her more than anything else.' The fire roared, and a log cracked.

'I blame myself, I should never have let her go,' he said. 'I don't know what to do, sir,' added Rishaan's father. 'There doesn't seem to be any point to anything. Nothing seems to be worth the effort.'

The old man nodded. He too had lost his wife early in life, and his beloved brother. It had taken him years to get over it. 'I lost myself in work; in fact, I worked too hard,' he said. 'When your mother died, and shortly later your uncle, I just could not stand the silence. I had to fill every waking moment with thoughts about work, about building and expanding. The nights were the worst, though. I hardly slept. I could only sleep when exhaustion took me.'

'I know the nights are the worst. I have Rishaan to distract me, but when I'm alone...' His train of thought trailed off.

They sat in silence for a while. His father's sadness got to Rishaan, and he wept. He tried to keep quiet; he wanted his father to talk more. He decided he had better go to bed and left.

That night, as he lay in bed, the big full desert moon shone into his room and filled it with a sad blue tint that made everything seem colourless. It was cold outside, the temperature dropping to below zero as the desert quickly cooled off and the cloudless sky let the heat flow into space.

A firefly flew into his room, which surprised Rishaan as he lay there. He was sure his window was closed. Then another and another until a large group of fireflies were in the room. He watched in fascination as the swarm circled at the end of his bed. They started to make a form, it looked like a human shape, and then it seemed to look more clearly like his mother. Rishaan though he must be dreaming. The fireflies kept flying, but the shape they made looked as if she was sitting on the bed.

Rishaan was scared at first but the face of his mother looked so familiar and friendly, and she was looking at Rishaan and smiling. Eventually, Rishaan plucked up his courage and asked 'Mother?'

The image smiled.

'Are you okay?' Rishaan asked.

The image smiled again, and then it spoke. It made no sound, but Rishaan could read her lips. 'I love you,' she said.

'Are you okay?' he asked.

She spoke again, and again no sound came out. Rishaan looked puzzled, so she spoke again. This time he could see what she was saying. 'I will always be with you,' she said.

The fireflies started to swarm again, and the shape of his mother slowly disappeared. The flies swarmed through the room, then left through the closed window. Rishaan buried his face in the pillow and cried.

Downstairs, Richard stared into the fire for a long time. Eventually the Captain spoke. 'You need to keep busy; it's for the best. Time heals everything, but till then you need to be distracted.' Rishaan's father nodded, but he did not look convinced.

The next day, Rishaan and his father had breakfast out on the veranda and watched some cattle being herded, as Shelly rode her horse around and played the cowgirl. They had just started a chess game when his grandfather came out.

'There's a call for you,' he said. 'It's the President.'

Rishaan's father was only on the phone for a few minutes, but soon they were packing their bags and making plans to head to Washington. The Captain arranged for a car to take them to Denver, where a train would take them to Washington. Within an hour, everything was ready.

Grandfather met them on the veranda as they left and he hugged them both.

'Take care of your father; he needs you more than you know,' he said to Rishaan. Then he turned to Richard. 'Your country needs you, your President needs you,' he said. 'We are all proud of you.'

The servants had already packed the car, and Rishaan was surprised to see Shelly in the car as well.

'We are going to London!' she shouted, and if she had her gun with her, she would have shot a hole in the roof of the car.

'Her parents are in London, so I promised to escort her back. Anyway, I think she has worn my father out,' said Richard.

Rishaan sighed; it would be a long sail back across the Atlantic.

'Funny thing about England,' she said. 'The English don't allow girls to carry guns – even if they are concealed!'

They left in a cloud of dust for the long journey to Denver. They would stay the night and then take the two-day train to Washington. Rishaan was glad his father was being distracted. He wanted to tell him about what was probably his dream last night, but he decided not to. It would only make him sad.

The car bounced around on the dirt road until it hit the better-travelled route 70. After a long nine-hour journey, they reached Denver. They stayed at a hotel near the station and caught an early train to the East Coast.

They stopped over in Chicago and then headed down to the Capitol, arriving late at night three days after they had left. America sure was a big country, thought Rishaan.

The next day his father had an appointment to see the President, and Rishaan had spent the last three days lobbying his father into taking him with him. He had successfully worn his father down with a combination of pleas, promises and downright begging. Shelly was locked up in the hotel, guarded by a heavily tipped member of the hotel security.

They entered the office of President Franklin Roosevelt, and the President was sitting on a couch in the Oval office. He did not stand up, and Rishaan noticed a wheelchair set to one side. They shook hands and the president motioned for them to sit down.

'I was so sorry to hear about your wife, Julia,' said the president. 'I knew her; she had interviewed me once. A bright woman, very smart.'

Rishaan's father nodded. 'Thank you, that means a lot to me.'

'I remember that you have a gift for languages,' said the president to Rishaan. 'I, on the other hand, have none. Never have been able to master the craft. I tried to learn Spanish once—an abysmal failure,' he said.

The president nodded to one of his aides, and Rishaan was led out of the room.

'Sorry, lad, but I have to talk some confidential stuff with your father.' Rishaan didn't even dare look disappointed; he had promised his father to be on his best behaviour.

The aid took him outside, and he sat on a bench. The corridor was busy, as aides either walked quickly or ran from one place to another. It seemed like the hub of the world, but so far away from the troubles in Germany.

'We are under a great deal of pressure to remain neutral,' President Roosevelt began. 'A great deal,' he repeated, to add emphasis. 'The people are tired of war, and tired of the antics of the Europeans who get themselves into their troubles and expect us to dig them out. We are still recovering from the horror that was the First World War. I don't want to see innocent American boys – and it's always the young that get caught up in these things - must go through this again. It's costly in human life and it's bad for prosperity.'

He paused for a while, deep in thought. 'However, I think Hitler is a maniac that needs to be controlled. I know the folks in Britain, France and some other countries agree with me, but back here, thousands of miles away, Hitler is not as feared as he should be.'

Rishaan's father nodded. 'I agree Mister President,' he said. 'Until Hitler does something that really crosses the line, America has little choice but to remain neutral. I agree that Europe should solve its problems and rely less on American intervention. However, I fear, like Winston Churchill, that Hitler is a mad dog whose bite is worse than his bark. He may be just a sabre rattler, but inaction on our part will only embolden him. I fear that there will come a day when he will have to make good on his rhetoric, or lose face among his fraction. He may be digging himself into that hole, as he has little else to offer.' The President nodded. He seemed to get lost in thought.

Rishaan sat patiently outside but his curiosity was killing him. When he thought no one was looking, he went over to the closed door and looked through the keyhole. He had hardly managed to focus when a strong hand grasped his shoulder. An army guard wagged a gloved finger at him, and led him back to his chair. Rishaan cursed under his breath. Why could he not stop getting into trouble?

The President continued, 'I want you to be my eyes and ears in London. Not the official line, but I need to know the politics that goes on between the lines. I need to know what is going on in Britain. I know that Prime Minister Chamberlain is trying to keep the peace, but his efforts seem naive and very optimistic. I would like to have contact with Churchill but he is considered a warmonger among the anti-war movement here in the US. Hitler and his cronies use Churchill as a symbol of America's lack of neutrality.

'I understand from Churchill that he has had contact with your son. Apparently, your son is quite the code breaker.' He leaned over to make his point clear. 'Use your son and Churchill to keep me informed, not about what is being said, but what is really going on. I hope that this will all blow over. Hitler came to power by creating and promoting false fear about the Bolsheviks and the Jews. However, once the German people get tired of him, they may get rid of him for us, and that will be that.'

'We can only hope, Mister President. Churchill has stood alone for a long time, warning of the danger of Hitler, but the British people are tired of war. They expect more from their politicians now, and they want peace.'

The president nodded.

Just then, one of the president's aides burst into the room. 'It's news from Europe, sir. Hitler has invaded Poland!'

War

THIS IS THE BBC CALLING:

'We have a clear conscience; we have done all that any country could do to establish peace. The situation in which no word given by Germany's ruler could be trusted, and no people or country could feel itself safe had become intolerable ... Now may God bless you all. May He defend the right. It is the evil things we shall be fighting against—brute force, bad faith, injustice, oppression, and persecution—and against them I am certain that the right will prevail.'

Neville Chamberlain, Prime Minister of Britain

Kurt Huisman was woken from his bunk early on the morning of 1 September 1939. He knew something was going on from the secretive behaviour of the officers the previous day, but as a simple nineteen year old ship's gunner on a German Navy training ship, he would never know what was planned until it was happening. He had already felt that the ship had slipped its moorings that evening, which was unusual, and the ship was not under full steam. It was as if they were trying to sneak out of the port of Danzig. He was ordered to full action stations, which for him meant behind the guns on the forward bow. The officers ordered everyone to be quiet. Kurt was used to these exercises; he had trained many a gunner himself. But this was different—he could feel it. The forward gun of the training ship Schleswig-Holstein was crowded and hot and Kurt was still a little disoriented from lack of sleep. Everything was cast in a dull red light, which meant they did not want to be detected by other ships or from land.

The last few days had been easy. The ship was in Danzig as part of a ceremonial visit and they had little to do. Now the officers were hissing orders at everyone, but Kurt could not figure out what was going on. Soon the ship stopped again, and Kurt could hear the anchors being deployed and the ship was still and eerily quiet. Everybody was at their posts but nobody said a word. Orders were given to load the guns, and this made Kurt nervous. What was the plan, what were they doing? He could see that the officers were tense and uneasy. The crew and officers sat in silence for what seemed like hours. Then one officer came over to the gun crew and whispered, 'When I give the signal, you fire and keep firing.' Kurt could not understand it. Usually when they did target practice it was in open sea. Then they often used duds; now they had loaded live ammunition.

It was dark outside and he could see very little from his gunner's compartment. They must still be somewhere in the port of Danzig, but he would follow orders, whatever he was told. He just adjusted the levers to lower or raise the gun on command from the gun aimer, and pulled the lever that fired the shell. He tried to think what it was they were going to be shooting at, but could only think it must be the Polish fortress at Westerplatte. This cannot be, he thought, Germany is not at war with Poland.

Then, at 4:47 on the 1st of September, the officer shouted 'FIRE!' Kurt pulled the lever that, unknown to him, would be the first shot in a conflict that would first entangle Europe, and then entwine the rest of the world in global war.

Rishaan, his father and Shelly left for Europe the next day, flying to the Azores, then to Ireland and then from there to

London. Richard had told Rishaan they would not be staying in London; they would move out to Chelmsford Hall – their country 'pile.' Rishaan loved Chelmsford Hall but he instinctively knew that his father was trying to get him away from any trouble that might be coming to London. Everybody feared the planes and the bombs.

Set in beautiful English countryside, Chelmsford Hall rested in the lap of the Dernham Valley. Established many centuries before, it was first a medieval settlement. Later, a lord built a small castle there, and then a small market town built up round it. It stayed small, as the lords that followed turned it into a large residence and built small residences around it. It became popular later as a rural escape from the busy city of London and the pomp of the aristocracy. This was mainly due to the excellent trout fishing that in the secluded river that meandered along the valley bottom. Due to its location, the area was one of seclusion and privacy.

It was where the shackles of social restraint were left at the gatekeeper's inn, and one was free to talk openly and network as guests of the owner of the house. It was for networking that Rishaan's grandfather had bought the estate and used it for socializing when in England. It was becoming part of the language of business and parliament that, when things needed to be sorted out politically but the official routes were not working or would take too long, then they would 'go down to Chelmsford.'

It was an unassuming main building, surrounded by cottages that were renovated with the latest conveniences. They all had telephones that connected them to a local operator; the rooms had running hot and cold water with their own toilets.

Most of them even had radios, and in the main building, there was a cinema that played the latest American films. It was also a complex of buildings that had grown and developed over a long period. The Captain would joke that the only person who had truly known every nook and cranny died 400 years ago, and since then things had been changed so much even he would not recognize the places and rooms.

An architect once offered to map the complex for the Captain, as part of a renovation, but he declined, saying it was like a lady, and a lady needs her secrets.

The two things Rishaan liked best about his bedroom were the view of the valley and the fireplace. The view of the valley was spectacular, but the best thing was that the Royal Air Force would use the valley for low flying practice. Big John owned most of the valley and had given permission, even though some local farmers had complained that it worried the cattle and sheep. This had at first been the case, but now they just munched on as the Hurricanes and Spitfires buzzed around. Rishaan loved watching them fly around and dreamed one day of flying one himself. They were so beautiful, so perfectly designed. There was an organic logic to them that looked to be a statement of perfection. They could not be better than that. The fact that they were better looking than the German Messerschmitt seemed to confirm to Rishaan that they were on the side of right. Secretly, he almost wished for a war so he could fly one in combat.

Then the open fire was wonderful. After a day out playing in the valley shooting rabbits and fishing, it was the best thing ever to get back to the house and matron had put his supper next to the snapping, crackling fire. It was the Christmases they spent at Chelmsford Hall he would remember the best. Family and friends, and the occasional famous guest, would fill the cottages. Errol Flynn, the film star, once stayed there, as did the Duke of York. There was always something going on in that unhurried time between Christmas and New Year.

It was not long, however, before Rishaan was beginning to dislike the quiet of Chelmsford Hall. He considered stealing the Bentley and driving it to London, but he knew his father would have a fit, and he did not want to cause any more trouble. His father was missing Rishaan's mother just as much as he was. Rishaan did not want to be the problematic son.

He had explored every room in Chelmsford Hall and found neither ghosts nor secret passages. He had found some photographs, one of which had been torn in half. On the back it listed the people in the picture, including one called, mysteriously, the 'photographer'. However, he was in the part of the photograph that was missing.

The other people were friends and family, people he knew. He wondered why it was torn, and why was the photographer on the torn bit, and why was he not named? Was he unknown to the people in the picture? Was he a professional photographer? If so, why would he be in the picture in the first place?

It was intriguing, but not exciting, and Rishaan soon bored with it and tossed the photograph back onto the pile of books and papers where he had found it. He looked out of the window as the day started to end and watched three Spitfires fly across the horizon, heading straight toward Europe. He wished he were old enough to be a pilot. He was audacious enough to lie about his age, but nobody would believe a twelve-year-old would be eighteen. He could fly a plane, though; his grandfather had shown him when he was in Arizona.

Then, to his surprise, he saw his father pull up at the front door, jump out and rush into the house. He ran up the stairs and into his room, calling James to come and help. Rishaan ran to his father's room and watched him.

'Pack for two weeks, James,' he called, 'and quickly; I have a flight to catch!'

'Where are you going, Father?' asked Rishaan.

'Not me, us!' his father said. 'Pack your bags, Rishaan, we are going to see the Canary!'

Before Rishaan knew it, they were on a flight to Spain, with a short stay in Paris. From France they flew to Gibraltar and then changed flights to Italy and then Germany. Rishaan was asleep when they landed in Berlin. He was whisked to the hotel, where he slept till the next day.

Germany had changed. He looked out of his hotel window and saw soldiers in the street. There were Nazi flags and posters hanging everywhere. Across the street, one of the shops had been boarded, upon which the word 'Jude!' and a star had been daubed. People appeared to hurry around; they seemed anxious, even afraid. A group of young soldiers, at least Rishaan thought they were soldiers, were boisterous and shouted and played around. They hurled abuse at some old men, pushing one over and laughing. Nobody did anything, and the old man got up and hurried on. Rishaan was surprised and wondered if he should call the reception desk and ask them to call the police. This was not his country, and he hesitated, but he decided to call anyway. The man at the desk was polite, as all hotel staff are, but he was dismissive of Rishaan, and even though he said he would investigate it, Rishaan knew nothing would be done. Rishaan found his father in the hotel restaurant and joined him for breakfast. Through the hectic race to get to Berlin, Rishaan had forgotten about his remark about seeing the 'Canary'.

'Who is the 'Canary'?' he asked.

Admiral Wilhelm Franz Canaris sat in the garden of his house in the suburbs of Berlin. It was a sunny afternoon, but the leaves on the trees were already turning, ready for the autumn winds to blow them into his garden. Canaris lamented about his gardener, who he had to let go because he was Jewish. He was a good man, and a good gardener.

The neighbour's children laughed and ran around and it was a joy to watch them, but Canaris still felt heavy-hearted. There was so much to do, so many things going wrong. He was head of the Abwehr, the German intelligence, and he was one of the few people who had a clear view of what was going on in Germany. He also knew that he would have to make a choice, and that choice would be soon. He needed to know if he had support among his colleagues at the Abwehr, and among the allies in Britain, France and America. It would be dangerous. Hitler had already ransacked his offices because he wanted to make sure Canaris's army officers would not warn their Polish officer comrades about attacks.

Most of the German civilians were ignorant of the terrible things that were happening in Poland, the unlawful deeds taking place in the name of the German government. He knew, despite his initial support of Hitler, he would have to do something about it. He hoped Hitler would unite a troubled

Germany, decimated by WWI, and save Germany from the communists in the east. This had been the case, but now Hitler was now a greater evil himself. His hopes that Hitler would mature into his role as leader were dashed. Canaris decided he wanted to relax. It had been a long week, and he could not carry this entire burden all the time. He watched the children play and enjoyed the last day of the summer.

Erika looked at her husband from the kitchen window. She was glad he was relaxing. He had been working too hard in these troubled times. She loved him because he was a brave man. He was a gentleman, who treated all with respect. He was also a brave man, who had been in many adventures.

Erika brought out some lemonade for her husband and the children, so they all came and sat in the grass next to the admiral.

'Tell us a story,' said one of the boys. He knew the admiral and always loved his tales of adventure. All the other children joined in and shouted for a story.

'Yes Wilhem, tell them a story.' said Erika.

The admiral smiled. It would be a nice distraction. 'I was once an intelligence officer on a ship in the German fleet, just at the start of the Great War,' he said. 'Ah, yes, the SMS Dresden, a great ship. We were being attacked by the British down by the Falklands, which is way down south, so far south the next land is the Antarctic. The British managed to sink all the other ships in our fleet but we managed to escape. We had turbine engines and could get up to 20 knots. It was a fine ship.

'Twenty-two hundred German sailors were killed or drowned in the encounter, including Admiral Spee and his two sons. A further 215 survivors were rescued and ended up prisoners on the British ships. Most of them were from the Gneisenau, nine from Nürnberg and 18 from Leipzig. There were no survivors from Scharnhorst.

'We were on our own out there but not defeated and for nearly a year we disrupted trade and evaded the British. The British have always had a better Navy than us, because they are an island, and Germany has few good harbours. Anyway, it was tough times, as we could not return to Germany, and we were on rations.

'One day we saw a French ship the RMS Ortega, with food and money and coal for the boilers. So we chased her. They did a great job of running from us; they managed to get their ship up to 18 knots, but we could do 20 knots! Slowly we got closer and closer. We aimed our guns and fired a warning shot – we didn't want to sink her, we needed her provisions!

'But they were crafty sailors and kept their stern to us all the time. Try as we might, we could not approach her broadsides. She kept running and ran into the uncharted channels of Nelson Strait, which were too shallow for us. They sailed right through; some people in small boats rowed ahead to take soundings, to make sure the water was deep enough.

'They succeeded eventually in working their way through nearly one hundred miles of the narrow and tortuous Smyth's Channel and emerged into the Straits of Magellan. After that, they navigated to Rio de Janeiro without even having a scratch on their plates.

'So we were stuck, and later we tried to hide from the British, but they found us at Robison Crusoe Island. We were trapped – no fuel, nothing.

So I got in a boat and went over to the British to discuss terms of surrender. Of course, I took my sweet time getting over there and tried to be as pompous and formal as possible. While I was buying time, the captain of the ship prepared to get all the crew off and scuttle the ship her by detonating the main ammunition magazine, so it would not fall into the hands of the enemy.'

The children sat around the admiral, the mouths open and their eyes wide in awe.

'I kept the British captain talking until one of the lookouts called that the Dresden was sinking. I hoped that most of the crew would escape, but we were captured and sent to Chile, where we were kept as prisoners of war.'

'Where is Chile?' asked a child.

'It's in South America,' said the Admiral. 'It's a nice place; I learned to speak Spanish there. Many of the sailors who were prisoners there decided to stay after the war and live there. I, however, decided to escape, and I made my way back to Germany pretending to be a Spaniard. I even grew a moustache! I even went through England, pretending to be a seaman. That's how desperate I was to get back to the fatherland.'

Erika laughed, 'He looked very handsome.'

The children laughed, and the admiral rolled up a piece of napkin and placed it under his nose.

'Now you look like Herr Hitler,' laughed Erika.

'Then I shall shave it off immediately,' said the admiral. Erika looked at him disapprovingly, not that she was a fan of Hitler—far from it—-but she knew that they were living in dangerous times, and her husband had to be more careful than anyone. Even among children. She knew her husband considered the Nazis to be thugs and a disgrace to Germany, but they did not talk about it. It scared her.

'Come on children, let the admiral rest,' she said. They all complained but did as they were told and left the admiral to enjoy the remains of the day. Erika smiled at the admiral and kissed his forehead, then left him to his thoughts.

Those were exciting times in South America, he thought. Maybe it was time to take risks again. It was time to meet the American. He unfolded a piece of paper he had in his pocket. It was a receipt from a clothes shop in Belgium. He took out a pen and wrote some numbers down.

Rishaan's father looked out of the window of their chauffeur-driven Mercedes Benz as they drove down the Unter de Linden Boulevard. He had heard a lot about Admiral Canaris and was eager to meet him. He also knew he had to be very careful. They had arranged to meet 'by accident' at a children's party held in the neighbour's house. That's why he had brought Rishaan along as a decoy. He did not want to get any information from Canaris; there were more subtle and discreet ways of doing that. He wanted to size up the man. Was he the real thing?

Canaris had created a scare earlier in the year by leaking information to the British that Hitler was making plans to invade Holland and use their airfields to bomb Britain. This caused a huge panic among the top British military and politicians. The rumours turned out to be false, but it had the effect that Canaris was looking for and that was that the British would take Hitler more seriously as a threat. This had intrigued Churchill who now wanted to find out more about

Canaris. Rishaan's father knew that the reason he was in Berlin was because Churchill had requested the neutral Americans to contact Canaris. The Americans also wanted to remain neutral, so it had to remain a secret.

They drove through the expensive suburban area. Life seemed normal here, almost tranquil, as the autumn leaves started to turn and fall.

Rishaan's father told Rishaan to listen carefully to what he had to say, as they approached the house. 'We are going to a party at a friend of mine, he is a wealthy industrialist. Don't let anyone know you understand German. I know how you like to show off but it's important you pretend you don't understand anything that is being said.'

Rishaan smiled, it sounded like fun.

'I will be meeting a German gentleman there and I will need to talk to him for a while. So you keep yourself busy and try to distract everyone,' Rishaan nodded. This was great fun. He would be seeing his father at work as a spy!

Canaris sat in his parlour with Rudolf Bamler, one of his officers from work. Canaris did not trust Bamler; he was a member of the Nazi Party, so Canaris kept him on a short leash. He knew that Bamler was reporting directly to Himmler. Everything Canaris said or did, Bamler reported to the Nazis.

'How is the coffee?' asked Canaris. Canaris had invited Bamler to his home so that he would witness Canaris had 'accidentally' talked to the American at a children's party. It would look innocent and would probably be forgotten. But in case it became an issue he could have Bamler as proof. He knew that Bamler did not speak English.

'Excellent, Admiral. Good coffee is so hard to come by these days.'

'I know, it helps to have contacts in Spain and South America,' he said.

Bamler smiled. He felt a bit awkward; he did not know why Canaris had invited him to his home, something unusual in the German hierarchy. He also felt a bit intimidated by the admiral. He was a legend among his staff and greatly respected. However, he felt that the admiral was holding him back. He needed to get his trust, so maybe today would be a breakthrough.

'It is good of you to come, Bamler,' said the admiral. 'I like to get to know my staff on a more personal level. Especially staff I have ambitions for.' The admiral did not intend to promote Bamler any further than where he was now. He was saying it purely to keep Bamler loyal.

'Thank you admiral,' said Bamler.

'Unfortunately, I have a double appointment today: my neighbour Herr Schmidt, the industrialist, has invited me to his children's party. We are both invited. You would do me a great Favor in going with me.'

'Of course admiral.' Bamler was pleased. Finally, his career was moving again.

'Welcome admiral!' the industrialist greeted Canaris. He was one of the few adults at the party who was not wearing some sort of uniform. Even some of the children wore a uniform.

'You have a beautiful house, Herr Schmidt. I dare say better than mine,' said the admiral. 'This is Lieutenant General Rudolf Bamler, a member of my staff.'

'Welcome! Please make yourself at home; there are drinks and cigars for the gentlemen. Food is in the dining room. Help yourself.'

Bamler looked at the food and saw the expensive drinks and cigars and gave Canaris a quizzical look. 'You would not think there was a war going on,' he mumbled. Canaris smiled.

'Ah look – there is my American friend,' announced Schmidt, and greeted Rishaan and his father at the door. Rishaan made himself busy playing with the other children. They all found him fascinating, as they soon found out that he lived in England and was half American. They tried their imperfect English, which led to much hilarity, and Rishaan found it very difficult not to let on he could speak German.

They started playing a game, the rules of which, despite his German, seemed to elude Rishaan. He did understand, however, that if you lost you were no longer an 'Aryan'. One child, who was dressed in the uniform of the Hitler Youth, looked scornfully at Rishaan. His father was a diplomat, he had travelled a lot like Rishaan, and he spoke fluent English.

'It seems that you English are trying to ruin everything,' he said, interrupting the other children.

'Why is that?' asked Rishaan.

'You are all ignorant of the Jews and the Communists. We Germans must live with it every day; we are on the front line.'

'Well, I'm half English so I guess I'm only half ruining it,' said Rishaan.

The blond child looked at Rishaan with disgust. 'You British should leave us alone,' he said, getting angry. 'Let us sort out the Poles and the trouble-making Czechs. It's all none of your business. If we do not take a stand and be strong, we will have the Bolsheviks on us, and then where will you be?'

Rishaan decided it was wise not to say anything. The Hitler Youth cadet looked like he was about to spit, but seemed to change his mind, and left.

'Don't worry about him,' said a child. 'He is very serious.'

'And his father is even worse.' said another.

One child said to another in German, 'They say he told the local police that one of their servants was part Jewish. They came and took him away.'

The mood had changed and the children talked among themselves. Rishaan followed the conversation.

'I've heard that the Americans are a simple people,' said one child. 'They do barbaric things like lynch people in public. I once read that they lynched a man in Texas; they even cut his fingers off to stop him from escaping.'

They both looked at Rishaan, and then went on to play elsewhere.

Rishaan's father was talking to the admiral and Bamler but the conversation was difficult. He had been told that Canaris could speak fluent English, but his English was basic. It made for a simple conversation. Bamler spoke nothing at all. He seemed irritated at the noisy children and frustrated that he could not speak English, so eventually he made his excuses and left.

'Well, thank God he's finally gone. It was exhausting trying to talk like an idiot,' said the admiral, his English improving considerably.

'Oh, I see,' said Rishaan's father.

'If they know I speak English well, they will distrust me. They are a very suspicious lot; they don't like people who have skills. It makes them feel threatened.'

Schmidt came around with some drinks. 'Would you like some Schnapps, gentleman?' he asked in English.

'I mind not, yes,' said Canaris

They went out into the garden for some privacy. As they talked Canaris pointed at things in the garden, giving any casual observer the impression they were talking about gardening.

'We in Germany are very concerned about the way things are going. We were very concerned about the Bolsheviks and we thought Hitler might help as a deterrent. But he has gone too far and I am convinced he will never be satisfied with a status quo. I already have some officers who are willing to work with me to try a coup, but we are too few yet and Hitler is too popular with the public. There is no popular support yet. We must be patient. Also, we do not trust Chamberlain, the British Prime minister, to stand up to Hitler. I sent one of my staff, Ewald von Kleist-Schmenzin, to talk to the British government, but only Churchill would listen.' Canaris grew more serious. 'I believe Hitler to be a very dangerous man. He is killing priests and Bishops in Poland! He could be insane, probably from being gassed during the Great War.'

Canaris looked around, and then slipped him a small piece of paper. They both nodded and returned to the house. Rishaan's father put the paper in his attaché case. He had not seen that Rishaan had seen what had happened. Rishaan was fascinated; it seemed like something out of a spy novel.

Reichsführer Heinrich Himmler and Bamler had lunch at a private restaurant the next day. Bamler was surprised at the attention he was suddenly getting from his superiors.

'Tell me Bamler, what did you and Canaris talk about?'

Bamler explained that Canaris was impressed with his work and suggested a promotion.

'Good for you, Bamler. I wish I could steal you away for my office, but I need you at the Abwehr; you are my eyes and ears there.'

Bamler smiled. He knew that the Nazis and Himmler were the true power base in Germany. If he ever wanted to get ahead, he needed to build his network there. He told Himmler about the rest of the day and meeting the American.

'Tell me more about the American.' said Himmler, as if it did not really matter that much.

'A diplomat, however he did not speak any German, and Canaris spoke English, but his English was not very good. The conversation was simple and banal. I got bored and left soon after.'

This piqued Himmler's curiosity, but he let it be for now. He did not want Bamler to think he was suspicious of Canaris. He knew Canaris inspired fierce loyalties from his staff. He had thought that Canaris was quite gifted in languages; it seemed strange that his English would be so poor. Or did he want it to seem that way? And if so, why? He made a mental note to check on Canaris's file to see if his English was indeed that bad.

Back at the hotel, Rishaan's father had a lunch meeting with an American colleague from the embassy, but it was boring talk on an exhibition about American – German relations being organized in Bonn, so Rishaan made his excuses and went back to his room. There was another reason he wanted to be alone; his curiosity about what was on the piece of paper was killing him.

At the room he found the attaché case and quickly flipped through the documents. He knew what he was doing was wrong, and his father would be furious if he knew. He did not want to look at the other documents, just that slip of paper. He just wanted to see what kind of spy work his father was involved in. He found a slip of paper that looked like what he was looking for.

At a quick glance he saw there were several numbers written in pencil on what looked like a receipt: 24.31.45.34.12

It meant nothing. Maybe it was a code. He needed to study it but he did not want to make a copy. Rishaan had learned a trick to remember things and he tried it now. He imagined walking into his house in London. He imagined 24 pairs of shoes by the door. He looked at the staircase; it had 31 steps going up. He walked into the kitchen, there were 45 sets of knives and forks in the drawers. There were 34 plates on the table, and 12 chairs around the table.

Just as he was refolding it, he heard the key being turned in the lock, and his father walked in. Fortunately, Rishaan managed to shove the paper into his pocket before his father could see. His father was deep in thought about something and walked into the separate room. 'Have you seen my attaché case?' he called.

'Yes father, here it is,' said Rishaan.

His father grabbed the case, patted Rishaan on the head and said, 'I'm just going out. Don't get into any trouble, and don't forget your homework!'

Rishaan smiled. His father left and Rishaan's heart sank. He hoped that the reason his father was going anywhere was not because of the paper slip that he needed. He did not have the time to slip it back into the case. He held the piece of paper, and then slowly unfolded it. It was written in German, the handwriting seemed uncertain and hastily written.

There was a noise outside. He looked out of the hotel window onto the busy 'Strasse'. He saw his father leave the building and cross the street. Two men appeared and started to follow him, then a car pulled up beside them and the two men forced his father into the back of the car. It all happened in broad daylight, and the people in the street pretended to ignore it and went about their business, as if it happened every day.

Rishaan tried to shout to his father from the window, but he knew he would not be able to hear him. He ran out of his room, but by the time he got to the street the car was already speeding off. He ran after it as fast as he could, dodging the other traffic. Cyclists shouted at him to be careful, and a truck full of German soldiers swerved as it nearly hit him. He would not give up, and tried to follow the car as it sped off into the distance. Sometimes it would slow down, because of other traffic, but the distance between them was getting greater. Then the car stopped, and one of the Germans who had forced Rishaan's father into the car got out. He looked at Rishaan and started walking toward him. Good, Rishaan thought; he wanted to go where his father was going, so they could take him as well. He plucked up his courage and started walking toward the burly man. However, as he passed a shady alley, a hand reached out, grabbing him around the throat and mouth and dragging him into the side street. He tried to resist, but the white-gloved hand was strong. Somehow, he sensed it was a woman's hand, but she was strong and she was not letting go, and soon more hands grabbed him and dragged him through a door. He tried resisting, but then the woman spoke.

'Be still!' she hissed. Rishaan knew instantly she was an American.

He wanted to fight more, but he somehow knew that he should do what she said. They sat in silence in the dark room, and they heard someone run past down the alley. Soon after, it was quiet. It was dark but Rishaan could make out that, besides the woman, there was another man.

'I will now release my hand, but before I do you have to promise me you will not shout out or try to escape.'

Rishaan nodded.

'We are on your side; we are part of the German resistance,' she said. Then she released her hand. 'We saw what happened to your father. He was coming to contact us with some important information. We want to know how much he knows about us and what he had with him.'

'Who took my father? Where are they taking him?'

'It's probably the Gestapo. They will take him to be interrogated, but don't worry, America is a neutral country so they will be very careful. They will make up some story that your father was involved with something suspicious, but they will release him, probably tonight. It depends what he tells them...'

'He will tell them nothing,' said Rishaan, proudly.

'I'm sure,' said the woman, and she smiled. 'But more importantly, it depends more on what they find on him. He has an important note from a friend of ours that he was supposed to give us.'

'Was my father meeting with you?'

'Yes,' said the woman. 'We cannot stay here, it is dangerous. Come with us and we will take you to a safe place. Do not talk; we do not want to attract attention with your English.'

'I speak German fluently,' said Rishaan, and the woman seemed impressed.

'Still sein, dann,' she said.

The man slipped out, then came back shortly and said that the coast was clear, so they left and hurried through side streets until a car picked them up. They took Rishaan to a safe house on the outskirts of Berlin. It was already getting dark and Rishaan was getting tired and hungry. The American woman tried to be nice but she seemed nervous and agitated about something.

'Who are you and where is my father?' asked Rishaan.

'You are with friends,' said the American woman. 'We don't give out names, but you can call me Millie. We don't know exactly where you father is but you should not worry, he will be let free soon. We can only hope that they do not find the thing he was trying to give to us.'

Rishaan remembered the piece of paper that he had shoved into his pocket. While the woman was talking to one of the men, he pulled it out. It was strange. It seemed like a bill of sale for some articles. The heading was 'Foreign Excellent Raincoat Company', with a list of some articles and numbers behind them. He hesitated, but then decided that maybe he should give it to the woman.

'I saw my father get the note from, er, someone. I had pulled it out of his attaché case to look at it. I was curious. I should not have done that, it was wrong of me,' he said. He held it out for the woman to look at. 'It doesn't make much sense,' he said.

She swiped it from his hand. She studied it and then seemed hugely relieved.

'Yes, this is what we are looking for, thank God! 'She showed it to the other man, and they discussed it.

'What does it mean?' asked Rishaan.

'It means you did something wrong, but by accident, might have saved a few lives,' she said.

'It seems like a bill for some clothes, that's all,' said Rishaan.

'It's in code.' she said, and left it at that. 'We are watching the building where your father is being kept; as soon as he is let free we will take you to him. Rest, you have had a busy day.'

They gave Rishaan some food, and he sat by a fire trying to get warm. Soon, another man arrived who seemed to be her husband and they talked in German. They sat at a table and talked about the bill that was lying in front of them. Rishaan pretended to be asleep and they soon ignored him.

'What is it?' asked the man.

'The Foreign Excellent Raincoat Company is a cover for a spy we have in Brussels. He works for the GRU, the Russian military intelligence, and has a network throughout France and the Low Countries.'

'What do the numbers mean?' he asked.

Millie just looked at the paper. 'I don't know,' she said.

Meanwhile, elsewhere in Berlin, Claus Schiffer arrived home alone. He had been out socializing with the Nazi elite, but they bored him. He had a healthy dislike of fanatics. They were his clients, however, so he needed to show his face occasionally. He also needed to see what was going on. Who was saying what to whom? He poured himself a brandy, then he sat at his desk and pulled out five folders. These were the new assignments he had received, and he looked through them. They were the usual political suspects, liberals and dissidents that needed to be taken care of. Most of his assignments he delegated out to other agents. He made some notes and added them to the folders.

The last folder made him groan. This was classic Himmler being paranoid. The object was a boy. He hated assignments like this. Women and children were not the targets of an elite soldier. This was not professional. This is not what warriors do; this was the amateur work of thugs. This sort of stuff made him concerned about the staying power of the Hitler regime. On top of that, his contacts in London had done a lousy job and had exposed his network to scrutiny. He would have to punish them somehow.

He tossed the folder marked 'Rishaan Finch' on to his desk and took a sip of his whiskey. He would have to take care of this project himself. Why did he have to do everything? He grabbed his horsewhip and swiped a piece of dirt from his boots. He hated mess.

Richard Finch sat patiently in the dark windowless office of the Gestapo building. He smoked a cigarette and looked at the guard by the door in the most condescending way possible.

Two men walked in, one in uniform, the other in a dark suit with an oiled leather coat slung over his shoulder. Finch could not discern his features very well, as he sat hidden at the back of the room in the shadows. The uniformed man sat down at the table and started looking through his files. The suit lit up a cigarette, but said nothing. Trained in interrogation techniques, Richard Finch would have to make sure they knew he was not easily intimidated, and he had to take control of the situation. Their silence was an attempt to intimidate, so he met that with silence. He was not worried about what was going to happen. He was a diplomat and a citizen of a neutral country. The Germans had little respect for law, but they were not stupid enough to disregard international law or create a crisis. He was not that important.

He could kick up a fuss and demand to be released, but he knew it would be more interesting to find out why he was being held. He could only think of one thing: they were sending out a signal. They suspected he had contacts with the resistance. By taking him in for questioning, they were saying to the outside world, 'This man is being watched.' The questioning would be a formality; they had already achieved what they wanted to achieve.

'Why are you in Berlin?' asked the uniformed man.

'I don't think we have been introduced. What is your name?' asked Finch.

'Why are you in Berlin?' repeated the uniformed man.

'Why are you asking me?' asked Richard.

'I ask the questions here,' said the uniformed man.

'Unless you charge me with something, there are no questions to be asked. I am sure you are aware that I am an American with diplomatic status.'

'You are on German soil, Mr. Finch; I hope you are aware of that?'

'I have an appointment with the United States Ambassador to Germany at 6 o'clock; I hope you are aware of that. I am more than willing to assist in whatever you need, but you will have to tell me why you are asking me. Otherwise, I shall take my leave. If you hinder me in any way it will be reported as a violation of international law.'

The uniformed man smirked. 'Why are you being so difficult, Mr. Finch, do you have something to hide?'

'Why should I have anything to hide? Surely, America and Germany are on good terms. Wasn't Hitler recently Time Magazine's 'Man of the Year'? '

'So you will have no objection to telling me why you are in Berlin?'

'And you will have no objection to telling me why you are asking me.'

'Have you had any contact with German citizens during your stay?'

'Why do you want to know?'

'You are not answering my questions Mr. Finch.'

'Neither are you,' replied Finch.

He parried and dodged for a while, waiting for the uniformed man to ask the real questions, if they had any. He wanted to see what they were trying to get at, without giving anything away. The questions did not seem to be coming. Soon, a guard came in and passed a note to the shadowy figure at the back of the room. The man read it then came over and whispered something to the uniformed man. He nodded.

'Tell me, Mr. Finch, maybe this is a question you will answer - where is your son?'

The next day, Rishaan was woken early and told to dress. 'We are taking you to your father,' she said. 'He has been released.'

Rishaan jumped out of bed and dressed quickly. He had some bread and cheese with some tea and they left for the city centre on bicycles. As they arrived, it was raining, so Millie opened an umbrella and they walked the last hundred yards to an alleyway close to the Hotel.

'We wait here for your father to come out,' she said.

They waited a while, and then Rishaan saw his father come out into the main entrance and stand by the door.

'There he is!' shouted Rishaan, filled with relief.

Millie opened the umbrella and they walked to the hotel. As they got closer, Rishaan saw his father look at Millie and shake his head. Millie whispered to Rishaan, 'We cannot stop, there is something going on, we must walk on' and she held tightly to his arm. Rishaan did as he was told but looked back, confused, as they passed the hotel. His father was watching them, and he looked concerned.

They circled back to where they had left the bicycles and cycled a circuitous route back to their safe house. Rishaan was told to wait while they tried to safely contact his father and find out what was going on. It took several hours before the messenger came back with some news.

'Apparently your father was interrogated for some time. He is fine; they did not touch him. He is a neutral American and they don't want to provoke America. They started asking questions about you, what you have been doing in London. They were saying you have apparently been doing some couriering of secrets to a politician, Winston Churchill. You father told them nothing, but when he got back to the hotel the room had been ransacked. They had been looking for you, or for something.'

Rishaan felt his heart drop. Had he gotten his father into trouble because of the games he had been playing? He would have to learn to stop getting into trouble.

'Luckily they did not find anything,' said Millie. 'It was lucky that you had taken that piece of paper with you. They might not have been searching for it but it would have been hard for your father to explain away. You will have to stay with us for a while; your father does not trust the Germans. He will be all right, but you are a British subject as well as an American, and Britain is at war with Germany.'

The next two days were very hard for Rishaan, but on the third day his father suddenly turned up at the house. They embraced, and Rishaan launched into a well prepared and thought out apology for everything he had done. His father smiled and interrupted him.

'It's okay. It's the sergeant major's fault; I will be telling him a thing or two when I get back to London.'

'Have they interrogated you again, father?' asked Rishaan.

'No, but they are following me. They suspect that I'm collecting information for the president to help make a case about war with Germany and they are trying to stop me however they can. I am playing the innocent, of course, but their tactics have made it impossible for me to do anything constructive. I have passed my sell-by date here in Berlin. I am just being a good diplomat now, but I will return to London soon. You are going to Switzerland. That's where the Germans think you are going or are travelling to with friends. I refused to divulge more.'

'I want to go with you, Father,' said Rishaan, but Richard was having none of it.

'This is your doing, Rishaan,' he said, 'so you will have to face the consequences.'

Rishaan knew that when he was called Rishaan instead of Kit, his father meant business. 'Yes Father,' said Rishaan, in the most reluctant voice he could muster.

Soon Rishaan was on his way to Switzerland, but plans changed quickly and he was soon hidden on a farm near the German – French border. It seemed that the Germans were looking for him. It was time for a more radical approach.

England

THIS IS THE BBC CALLING:

It is with great regret that the Government announces that HMS Courageous has been sunk in the Western Approaches by German submarine activity. The survivors were rescued by the Dutch ocean liner Veendam and the British freighter Collingworth. Although the two escorting destroyers counterattacked U-29 for four hours, the submarine escaped.

A week later, Rishaan was hiding at a secret spot in a forest. He had been hiding in the bushes for what seemed like forever. This was the third night he had hid here, and the plane had not arrived. Millie told him that this was normal; they wanted to see if German soldiers were in the area, if the arrival date and time had been compromised. Only the pilot in England knew which of the ten dates and times that had been given would be the real one. Rishaan knew that it was getting close to the time, and there was no sound of any plane in the distance. It would be another wasted night. Rishaan could not wait much longer; he needed to get his information to Churchill as soon as possible. He was cold and tired.

Trying to keep still and quiet was wearing him down and in the dark, he felt sleep overwhelming him. In the woods, as he waited with his French friends, he could hear all kinds of noises: twigs breaking, birds calling, animals scurrying around. Millie whispered to him, 'I like it when we can hear the animals, that means there are no police around to disturb them. The forest is at rest tonight.' Rishaan smiled at Millie but he was uncertain about what was going to happen.

Millie had told him that the plane would land and immediately turn around and get ready to take off again. The landing would be difficult. With only a few torches as guides, the pilot would have to land more on faith than on any visual cues. It was not a full moon tonight, which would make finding the landing spot difficult and landing even more so. Rishaan had to run over and climb in the plane when the pilot signalled to him. The plane would take off immediately; they did not want to hang around. The Germans would probably come as soon as possible, but with a quick turnaround, they would only find an empty field, a few burnt out torches and the lingering smell of gasoline fumes.

Rishaan began to doze off. He was exhausted by the tension of the last few days and the wait for the plane. He did not care anymore about the dangers of the flight back. He would care, however, if the plane never even got to the landing field. It was a dangerous mission even flying this far into Germany. Then there was the even more dangerous flight back. Even if he could get into the plane and leave before the Germans arrived, they would have an alerted German air force waiting for them. Rishaan awoke, startled, as a plane roared overhead, scattering the frightened wildlife in all directions. The pilot had found the field but was coming in from the wrong angle. Millie and her friends scattered from their hiding places and started lighting the fires to mark the landing strip. The Spitfire buzzed around but it was clear he was having difficulty locating the field. Franz had told Rishaan the pilot would only make three attempts to find the field and land before aborting the mission. The plane did not have enough fuel to hang around too long, and certainly could not wait for the German Messerschmitt patrols to turn up for a fight.

Rishaan could see it was a Spitfire. It flew low again across the field, but could not land and pulled up to miss some trees and disappeared out of view. Rishaan knew that was his last attempt. The plane was gone. Strange that it was a Spitfire, they were only a one-seater aircraft - what was the point of sending that to pick up a passenger? Now the silence returned, more eerily than before, as the plane had scared away most of the animals in the forest. Rishaan looked at Franz; they both seemed uncertain what to do. It was now dangerous to stay here, as the Germans were sure to arrive soon.

'Let's go, we need to get out of here,' said Millie. Rishaan's heart sank. The mission had failed. He would not be able to get back to England soon. He knew that England would never risk another attempt; they had wasted enough resources on him as it was. The only way for him to get home now was to go to Switzerland and try from there, or down through Spain to Gibraltar. Both routes would take months and would be fraught with danger.

'Make sure you take everything with you. Do not leave anything behind that will give us away,' said Millie. She was being practical now; she had no time for Rishaan's feelings. Rishaan could find nothing. They had been careful, so now they left. Millie's friends left in different directions. They would all pretend to be poachers now, out hunting rabbits. Some even had freshly shot rabbits with them.

Just as they reached the forest road leading out of the forest, the Spitfire screeched overhead again and set in for a landing. Almost at the same time, headlights from a truck beamed through the forest. Judging by the speed of the truck, on such a night, it could only be the German police. Millie and her men scattered into the forest, leaving Rishaan behind. He had to make a choice - to run with Millie or make for the plane. He had only one shot, so he ran back toward the landing strip. Millie called out to him, but the roar of the Merlin engine on the Spitfire drowned out what she was saying. The Spitfire braked so heavily after landing that the plane nearly pitched over. As soon as the pilot was able to taxi, he skilfully spun the craft around and lined it up for take-off. The cockpit hood swung back, and the pilot jumped out, his hand holding a pistol. He had a large, waxed moustache, his face covered in a thin layer of oil and dirt. Rishaan waved his arms in the air, a signal that he was a friendly, and ran up to the pilot. 'Where is my passenger?' the pilot barked.

'I'm your passenger!' Rishaan shouted back.

The pilot cursed and slapped the plane with his fist. 'They sent me on this mission just to rescue somebody's kid?'

'Do you want to discuss this, or shall we get out of here?' shouted Rishaan. He was not going to lose his flight now just because he was a kid.

'Get in!' shouted the pilot. Rishaan did not get it at first, but then he saw that the Spitfire had been modified, and behind the pilot was a cramped space where he could climb in. Rishaan scrambled into the cockpit, the pilot pushing him so that he went in headfirst. The pilot jumped in the plane, revved the engine and pulled the cockpit shut. The truck containing the German military burst out from the forest onto the landing strip in front of the Spitfire, blocking its way. They started shooting and flashes of red light whizzed past the plane.

The pilot revved again and the Spitfire picked up speed. The pilot aimed straight for the truck, firing his Browning guns. The bullets ripped into the truck, shearing off the roof and hitting the driver, who slumped over, spinning the steering wheel, turning the truck over and spilling the German guards out onto the landing strip. The Spitfire roared up and took off, just in front of the overturned truck, striking the truck with its left landing carriage, which snapped off like a twig. The lame Spitfire limped into the air, followed by a rain of bullets from the soldiers below. Rishaan could hear the bullets clipping past, some missing, and some going through the duralumin skin of the fuselage. Clipping the tops of the trees at the end of the landing strip, the plane remained low, the pilot struggling to get the broken undercarriage back up into the wings, keeping the craft aerodynamic.

It took Rishaan a good ten minutes to get himself righted but when he finally got to look out, he saw that the pilot was flying low across the treetops. The dawn sun had already started to rise in the east, so Rishaan could orient himself. The pilot was flying straight back to England, which meant he had barely enough fuel. At least he was flying back home; Rishaan knew that if he was short on fuel he would make a dash for Switzerland instead. Rishaan found a helmet with an oxygen mask and a mike to talk to the pilot. Rishaan tried to talk but the pilot either could not hear him, or didn't want to. Soon Rishaan began to relax, despite the roar of the Merlin engine, which was probably waking every German between Dusseldorf and the North Sea. Here he was fulfilling a dream - to fly in a Spitfire. He marvelled at the shape and the speed of the aircraft as it sped at 370 mph across the hilly German terrain. Rishaan felt exhausted, and despite the cold, the drone of the engine was lulling him to sleep. A sharp command from the pilot brought him to his senses.

'That thing you are sitting on—it's a parachute. Strap yourself into it.' Rishaan struggled to figure out what strap went where, and was not finished before the Spitfire veered to the port side. The pilot gained some height then went into a shallow dive, flying over a road, what looked like one of Hitler's famous highways. Rishaan heard a clunk and the Spitfire gained height; looking back, he saw what looked like a bomb drop and land smack in the middle of an expensive German car that had Nazi markings. The car swerved, and veered off the road. The pilot gave a whoop!

'The bomb didn't go off!' shouted Rishaan.

'It wasn't a bomb, it was the empty fuel tank!' the pilot shouted back. Rishaan strained to see what had happened to the car, but it soon disappeared into the distance. He wondered if he would ever know what had happened.

The Spitfire sped on, clipping trees, roaring across the German countryside, then across what looked like the flat Dutch landscape, with ditches, small canals and windmills. Rishaan wondered about Wouter, if he was safe in Amsterdam. They were getting closer to home. The Spitfire started making unexpected noises—bangs, coughs, splutters—but kept flying. The pilot would occasionally curse and hit something on his flying panel, but the Merlin motor kept roaring, the noise deafening and excluding all else.

Soon the North Sea replaced the flat land as the Spitfire headed out toward England. The pilot felt more confident now and began to increase the altitude. The pilot seemed more relaxed, and more amenable to Rishaan. 'I want to get some altitude; it's safer. We don't want some Messerschmitts attacking us from above,' he said. 'I'm heading for the clouds for cover.'

It was cloudy and the dawn sun was giving dramatic lighting effects as the pilot dodged in and out of the clouds. Something seemed to have spooked him, but he did not respond to Rishaan's prompting. Rishaan soon saw some planes off to the east and behind them; he could not tell if they had seen them yet, as they kept entering clouds.

'They might be sending out a patrol to help us back, but I'm not counting on it,' said the pilot. 'We have a lame duck here. I think the undercarriage is damaged, we might have a rough landing. We will fly past the control tower once to see if they can assess the damage. I don't have much petrol left; we will have to make some snap decisions. If we can't land, then we will just have to jump.'

'I've jumped before,' said Rishaan. 'I've had training.'

The pilot turns around and looks at him quizzically. Then suddenly, as they leave the protection of a cloud, they almost fly straight into a huge Zeppelin. The pilot swerves instinctively, pulling the plane to the port side and up, just missing the top of the Zeppelin. Just as quickly as they had passed the airship, they disappeared again into a cloud.

'That was close!' shouted the pilot, as Rishaan watched the huge shape of the airship disappear again into the mist.

'That's why you came to pick me up. I have information for Churchill about how dangerous those Zeppelins are!' shouted Rishaan.

'Well, in that case...' said the pilot and he banked sharply. 'I can give it one good strafing – then maybe if we fly upside down the rest of the way, we might get some more petrol fumes into the engine.' Rishaan wasn't sure if the pilot was joking, but he knew he would soon find out.

The Spitfire emerged suddenly from the cloud and lined up at the back of the airship flying toward its tail. The pilot tried to fire his Browning guns but they fired only a few tracers then it seemed to block. The pilot hurled some obscenities as the plane skirted over the airship's back. As the plane passed over the nose, a roar was heard as a Messerschmitt flew across. The pilot swore some more.

'Okay, more than we can handle, we need to get out of here' he shouted, and he spun away and up, searching for some cloud to hide in. The Messerschmitt was having nothing of it and spun around to chase.

'The damage to the undercarriage is causing drag!' shouted the pilot. 'We are not flying as fast as we can, and using more petrol!'

The Messerschmitt seemed to sense the easy kill that was available and honed in. Rishaan could hear the buzz of its engines above the roar of the Merlin motor.

There followed a twisting and turning match, with the Spitfire banking and dodging at a frantic pace. Rishaan felt himself being thrown from one side to another, and then sometimes pushed down into his seat by g-forces that made him feel that his whole body was going to be crushed. The pilot then reared the nose of the Spitfire up into the air, spinning the kite onto its back in a loop, trying to get above the Messerschmitt and back down behind it. The looping made

Rishaan lose consciousness. For a few seconds he was somewhere else, a dreamland, back at Chelmsford Hall, but then he awoke again to the roar of the engine and the scream of the Messerschmitt as it dodged the Spitfire. The German pilot was too experienced to be out maneuvered by the lame-duck Spitfire. He spun around, strafing the British plane head-on. The bullets ripped across the starboard wing, debris hitting the pilot in his shoulder.

Then the Messerschmitt was gone, losing the Spitfire in the clouds. The pilot pulled the nose up to gain altitude.

'We are done for!' he shouted. 'The starboard wing is gone, it's starting to break up. We have no fuel left; you will have to jump! You go first, I'll keep the plane as steady as I can.'

The pilot turned and looked at Rishaan for a few seconds. 'I'm sorry,' he said.

The pilot yanked open the cockpit canopy and the cold and the rush of air blast in, pushing Rishaan into the back of his seat. He struggled to stand up and the pilot reached his hand out to help. Rishaan saw that he had been badly injured: his face was bleeding and his bomber jacket ripped and bloodied.

Rishaan hesitated at the idea of jumping out into mist. He could see nothing. He had little time to think about it, as the pilot flipped the plane and Rishaan fell out, head first. Blinded by the rain and the cold, and oil from the damaged plane, his hand groped for the cord to release the parachute. After what seemed like an eternity, the parachute opened, jerking him roughly. He had put on the parachute badly, and the parachute straps, twisted, dug into his skin. But they held, and for the moment he was safe. He could hear the Messerschmitt buzzing around, searching frantically for its easy confirmed kill. He could also just see the Spitfire.

It was the pilot's turn to jump. He put his hands on the sides of the cockpit to pull himself up, but a stab of pain from his injured shoulder stopped him in his tracks. He paused, regaining himself. For a second, he looked at the cockpit, and placed a hand on the dashboard. 'Goodbye old friend, I will never forget you,' he said, then heaved himself out of the cockpit, with a cry of pain, and fell into the mist around him. Pilotless, the Spitfire started a graceful roll to the port side, the starboard wing going up as if to wave goodbye to the pilot, as it rolled down into the mist and down to its last resting place in the North Sea.

Rishaan could see the pilot falling. He seemed to be motionless, as if unconscious, as he fell backwards through the cloud.

'Pull the cord!!' shouted Rishaan, but he knew the pilot could not hear him. The limp body of the pilot disappeared into the mist. Shortly after, Rishaan thought he saw the shape of a white circle appear, and then slowly disappear again in the mist. He hoped it was the pilot's parachute, but he was not sure.

Rishaan's fate was not much better than the pilot's. He was freezing and he could not stay conscious for much longer. But he did not know how far away the ground was, either, so he HAD to stay awake. And when he reached the ground, there was only the cold North Sea, probably miles from any coast, to greet him.

Then there was the silence. The Messerschmitt had left, maybe following the Spitfire down to confirm the kill. Now only the fog of the cloud surrounded him. After a few minutes, he started to hear another, unfamiliar sound. It was a slow drone, plodding and rhythmic, unlike that of a fighter plane. He could not make it out; maybe it was a ship. The white shape looked like the wake from a large steamer. He tried to steer the parachute in the general direction of the sound by pulling on the front cords of the parachute. Gradually the mist began to disappear, and it came into view. He was at a much higher altitude than he thought. He was looking down on the top of the German Zeppelin as it appeared like a phantom out of the mist. He tried desperately to steer his parachute toward the craft, but winds kept buffeting him, pushing him to one side, then pulling him back, sometimes even pulling him upwards.

Suddenly a gust caught him and he was pulled over the top of the Zeppelin. Pulling hard on his parachutes ropes, he landed awkwardly on the top of the airship. It felt very hard for what was basically a big balloon. The parachute collapsed, but then was filled again as a wind blew across the Zeppelin's spine. The parachute dragged him along the spine toward the large tail fins. Rishaan had to make a snap decision. Did he stay attached to the parachute that would surely drag him off the craft? Or should he unstrap himself and risk falling off the airship to his certain death. He struggled to unstrap, and realized that there was a quick release button. It was jammed, so he tried his hardest to get the mechanism to work. His fingers, blue and bloodied from the cold, had little grip. Suddenly there was a snap, and the parachute took off on its own in the wind, first wrapping itself around and then disappearing behind the tail fin. Free of Rishaan's weight, it flew upward, carried by the wind.

Rishaan held on tightly to the slippery outer skin of the airship. His cold wet hands were slowly losing their grip; he felt his dead weight gradually dragging him down the sloping side of the airship. He frantically struggled, but his struggling made him lose more grip on the canvas skin. His hands became wet, the feeling in his fingers numb from the cold. He felt one of his feet wedge against a metallic rib. It was too slippery to give him a push up; when he tried his foot would slip off, but it was enough to break his slide over the edge, giving him a little time to regroup and see what his options were. He still had a penknife in his pocket, but he could not reach for it. He needed both hands to stop himself from sliding. In addition, if he dug his knife into the skin of the airship, would it go pop like a balloon? The thought made him laugh to himself, and that made him laugh out loud. Here he was in a dangerous situation, and all he could do was laugh! The Zeppelin passed through some more clouds, drenching Rishaan more. He felt exhausted, and he knew he would not be able to hold on for much longer. There seemed little chance of getting out of this one. He tried kicking with his free leg to rupture the skin of the airship, but the thick canvas was too strong for him.

Then the airship passed out of the cloud into the blazing sun, warming Rishaan a little. Inside the Zeppelin, Rishaan's body was silhouetted on the canvas outer skin, betraying his presence. He saw that the rib he had his foot wedged on travelled the length of the airship. If he could figure out how he could move along the frame, he could maybe discover a route going up. He could not see anything, as the body of the airship curved away out of sight on both sides, but this was his only option.

He moved slowly. Sometimes he had more grip, sometimes it seemed that he was losing track of where the rib was. At one point, he managed to get both feet on some sort of grip, and he rested. He felt he was losing consciousness from exhaustion, so he knew he had to keep going. He slowly slid his foot forward, but the groove of the rib soon disappeared again and his foot slid off, making him nearly lose his grip on the side. He realized he could not slide back either. He tried to relax, but the wind was starting to buffet him now. Until now it had been blowing him into the side of the airship, but he could see that the craft was slowly turning, and soon the strong wind would be blowing along the side of the Zeppelin, and his tenuous grasp would be easily unlatched. He felt giddy; he was beginning to hear voices. He had to concentrate. The voices got louder, shouting. They were German voices. He felt a strong grip around his left wrist, and he was pulled upward along the frame to higher ground on the airship's back. The pull was dislocating his shoulder and the pain was excruciating, but it was saving his life, and that was all that mattered.

He looked up to see two Germans, one with a rope around his waist. They were both laughing, delighted that they had managed to rescue him. The older German aviator, who had risked his life to grab Rishaan, pointed at Rishaan. 'It's only a kid!' he shouted to his comrade, above the wind.

His comrade stared in disbelief. 'Come on!' he shouted. 'Let's get below – it's cold enough up there, let alone dangerous.'

They pulled Rishaan to his feet, and then they guided him to a porthole near the nose of the airship, almost like the blowhole on the head of a whale. Rishaan immediately felt the warmth inside the craft as he entered the hull of the airship and climbed down the ladder. Inside the Zeppelin was a cavernous hulk, with huge air bags filled with hydrogen, and all around were crew working. Rishaan climbed down with the soldiers and they took him across a corridor between the gas bags to another ladder that descended into the belly of the airship. The airmen guided Rishaan carefully but firmly toward the captain's gondola that was slung below the airship. The crew was busy controlling the ship, but all looked at Rishaan, fascinated.

'Where did you come from?' barked the captain. He was a tall man with a large white beard and a scar across his face. He seemed angry and irritated.

Rishaan knew he would have to think fast, or he still might be thrown overboard after all. 'Ich bin Rishaan,' he said, in German. He knew his German was good but not good enough to convince a German he was German. He would have to think fast. 'I am from Wallonia, the East Cantons, the German part of Belgium. My father is German and my mother is Belgium. I was with my father on a flight when we were attacked. I don't know by whom. I thought I saw two planes. It was all so confusing, we hid in the clouds. Have you seen my father? His name is Hans.'

The captain looked about at the people around him. They all shrugged their shoulders. They did not know what to make of it.

'Were you in the Spitfire?' one of the officers asked.

'He could not have been,' answered another. 'The Spitfire is a single-seater, as is the Messerschmitt.'

'Were you flying the Spitfire?' asked another, and some crew laughed.

'What's a Spitfire?' answered Rishaan, using all his powers to look the innocent youth.

The captain looked a bit bewildered and looked around at the crew. The first officer shrugged his shoulders. 'I guess we can't throw him back into the sea,' he said.

'Maybe we can drop him off in Belgium when we pass over it,' said the captain.

'But sir,' said a crewmember, 'we do not have permission to land in Belgium.'

'Who said anything about landing?' replied the captain and the crew laughed. The captain did not look as if he was joking, and the crew quieted.

There was a distraction that took the captain to the steerage, so Rishaan just stood there, shivering, wondering what to do next. He felt the warmth of the cabin slowly seep back into his body, as a puddle of water collected around his feet from his dripping clothes. The guard made him stand to one side as the crew got ready to make some change in direction, and it seemed he had become instantly forgotten and invisible.

He stayed there, quiet and unobtrusive, but keenly observing the activity on the deck. To one side, there was a row of screens like he had seen at the radar station at the beginning of the year with his father. That seemed like years ago, now. He could occasionally hear what the operators were saying. It was clear that what they were doing had nothing to do with the operation and flight (propulsion?) of the airship.

Edging over, trying to look more interested in the crew and the workings of flying than in the secrets of the radar station, Rishaan could just hear what they were saying. He could not make much sense of it. It was very technical and they spoke German rapidly. Suddenly, the captain yelled at them from across the deck,

'What do we need to do now?'

'We have completed the higher frequencies and found nothing,' said the operator.

'Do we need to go back again?'

The operator talked to his senior officer for a few seconds. 'No, we only need the higher frequencies; we know enough.'

'Okay, good, take her home, men,' shouted the captain. The captain put on his cap and charged off the deck, on to some other problem. As he stormed past Rishaan he shouted, 'Get a medic to check him out, then lock him up somewhere till we get back home.'

One of the orderlies that had saved him from the side of the airship grabbed his shoulder and marched him out of the deck. They walked again through the belly of the ship, and Rishaan spied a small biplane, tucked at the back, hanging from a hook. It looked almost like a toy, but Rishaan saw it was a real plane. It had no guns or other additions, and small stubby wings. It had what looked like a camera mounted from one side. It seemed to be used as a spy plane. Rishaan assumed it could be dropped from the airship, as there was a hole underneath the plane that it could fit through. He wondered if the plane could return to the airship later or would have to make its own way home. It looked amazing. He looked around to see if he could find anything else that would be useful to

Churchill. He kept himself focused on his mission; otherwise, he would have been too scared.

He was taken to a separate area, and one of the airmen came over and started asking questions about his hearing, and if he had any pain anywhere. Rishaan hurt all over, but there was nothing except bruises and bumps, and his fingernails were broken from clinging to the side of the airship. He had become a little warmer now and asked if he could have something to eat. Rishaan knew also that he would have to have a better story for when he got back to Germany, and maybe they had already radioed ahead, although he hoped that they were flying under radio silence to avoid detection. Well, at least he was not now swimming in the North Sea. Still, it would not take too long for the Gestapo to put things together.

Suddenly there was a huge bang as a bullet hit the metal frame next to Rishaan, splinters flying in all directions, scratching him and ripping his shirt.

'Kampfflugzeuge,' shouted the airman, and everybody ran to their battle stations, leaving Rishaan forgotten and to his own devices. Rishaan looked around for a place to hide, but there was not much to protect him in this large balloon. He ran back down the airship, dodging the other airman as they ran about. He ran to the small biplane at the back. He had no plan but maybe the cockpit would give some protection. He climbed in quickly and hid. There was chaos going on around him, but he could not see anything. All he could see were the basic controls of the craft and above him a lever, painted red. The lever was attached to some cogs that, once the lever had been pulled, would rotate and a grip around a hook that held the plane in place would be released.

'Achtung,' shouted an airman, who had just spotted Rishaan. He reached over and tried to grab Rishaan by the hair. Rishaan struggled, knocking the airman's hand away. The airman shouted over to others to help him, but another strafing by the fighter plane sent him running for cover. Rishaan decided that the only way out was to pull the lever. He grabbed it, and pulled as hard as he could but it was stuck. It descended an inch, letting the cogs turn a little, but stopped. Rishaan was just too small and light to get it moving. He tried again, jerking it down, gaining a little distance each time. He heard the airman shouting again, so he gave it one more pull. There was a snap, as the grip opened and the biplane appeared to hover in midair for a second, and then dropped down through the hole in the airship.

Rishaan was caught off guard and was left hanging onto the lever. He let go instantly, but was left falling through the hole, after the biplane. Fortunately, the biplane's wings slowed the fall of the craft and Rishaan fell faster, plummeting head-first into the cockpit, his legs pointing upward to the airship, as it disappears upward.

He fought to right himself. The cockpit was slightly bigger than that cramped cubbyhole in the Spitfire, but still it took him a full minute to right himself. The biplane seemed to be falling through the mist, and without a horizon, Rishaan had difficulty orienting himself. He tried to figure out the controls; they all seemed simple. Rishaan just needed to figure out how to get the engine running. Suddenly, the biplane fell out of the bottom of the cloud. To his horror, Rishaan saw that the biplane was diving nose forward toward the sea. Rishaan knew that the only way to get the plane to fly was to increase speed, but there were no instruments in this basic plane; everything seems stripped out. Instinctively he kept the nose down, increasing the speed of the plane as it hurtled toward the sea. He tried starting the engine, but nothing seemed to be working. As the plane gathered speed, the force of the air started to rotate the propeller, and Rishaan tried to get the engine to kick-start. Finally, Rishaan could wait no longer and pulled back on the joystick, and the plane slowly but surely pulled its nose up, finally righting itself just enough to skim over the sea surface. Rishaan tried the engine again, and this time the engine coughed and spluttered into action. He gave it full throttle but the plane seemed to have lost momentum, and began shuddering, a sure sign that it was reaching a stall.

'Come on! Come on!' shouted Rishaan, the engine screaming as he gave it full throttle. He felt forward motion but the plane was still sinking. He dared not pull back on the joystick, as that would only reduce the speed and then he would stall. The sea started to come closer and closer, the waves reaching up to grab the plane and pull it down. He could even smell the salt and the seaweed. Slowly, painfully, the plane started to climb and Rishaan gradually, gently pulled the nose upward. He figured out where the flaps were and when he was confident the air speed could handle it, he extended the flaps to gain more height. After what seemed like an eternity, the grasping waves were far below him; Rishaan banked the plane and using the sun as a guide, headed toward the northwest, the general direction of England.

He flew straight into another cloud, glad for the cover; he could hear gunfire in the distance above the roar of the biplane's engine. He hoped that he was keeping a true course toward England, but the cloud around him disoriented. The noise of the gunfire became louder and he heard other planes. He looked around, frightened. He didn't know what to do. The sounds were now coming from everywhere – even human voices shouting. Suddenly, he flew out of the cloud into a clear space, like an arena. Two Spitfires were attacking the giant airship. Smoke was coming out of the side of the frame and the nose of the airship was pointing downward, because it was either trying to escape or was badly crippled. It looked like a huge whale being attacked by sharks. Rishaan had to bank to avoid the balloon, and he shouted out, 'NO!' He was overwhelmed with emotion at the sight of such a majestic object being preyed upon, and in his tiredness, sobbed uncontrollably. Immediately, the clouds swallowed up Rishaan's plane again and Rishaan tried to keep control. He wiped the tears from his face, but they mixed with the oil, grease, and filth and stung his eyes. He just wanted to get back home now, back to England, back to his friends and the safety of Chelmsford Hall .

More quickly than he had expected, the white cliffs of Dover loomed up before him, and he flew safely over the top. He was back over land, except he had no idea where he was. He gained some more altitude, hoping to see the tell-tale sign of a landing strip where he could try to land. Suddenly a Spitfire flew up to him and the pilot looked at him for a few seconds. Rishaan laughed and waved frantically at the pilot. He had forgotten that the plane he was flying in was German, although it had no markings.

The pilot banked away and disappeared. Rishaan wished the plane had a radio of some sorts but he probably would not know how to operate it. He flew aimlessly for a while, not knowing what to do. He didn't see anything familiar. Churches, lakes, train lines, roads. Small villages. They all look the same from above. Suddenly he recognized Canterbury Cathedral, and he flew to it. From there he knew the roads and followed them. He could find his way back to Chelmsford Hall, and maybe there was a landing strip on the way. He flew low across the English countryside. It was a beautiful day, the sun now strong, clearing the mist on the fields. Despite the danger he was still in, Rishaan felt exhilarated, the emotional rush of being free.

It was the coughing of the engine, signalling that the petrol level was low, that brought him back to reality. There was only one thing to do. He was nearly home; he would land on the field in front of Chelmsford Hall. Soon Chelmsford Hall loomed up before him. He had never seen it from the sky before; it looked so small. He checked to see if the field was obstacle-free. Luckily, there were not many cows in the field and they would just have to get out of the way, so he banked around, and lined the plane up for a landing. He was not quite sure what to do about the undercarriage. He could not see any levers or controls to lower them and he could not see if they were fixed and already deployed under the wings. In the end there was nothing he could do. The plane flew over Chelmsford, knocking a chimney pot off. The children of Chelmsford ran out to see what was happening. All they could see was a tiny biplane flying erratically, and circling around.

As if timed perfectly, the engine coughed a few more times, gasping for petrol, and then died. The biplane landed heavily on its wheels, bounced, then landed back again heavily, breaking the wheels off, and the plane crashed onto its belly. It slid along the wet grass, crashing through the flimsy fence onto the gravel path driveway and smashing into the fountain in front of the main door, knocking the statue of Pan back into its upright position.

Rishaan could not believe it. He was still alive. After the dust settled, he climbed carefully out of the plane. He was stiff, bruised, everything hurt, but he could still walk. All the children of Chelmsford Hall were standing outside and watching in amazement. Ambrose stood at the door as Rishaan walked up to the group, smiled, then walked past the servants into the house.

'Park the car, will you, Ambrose?' he said.

Rishaan stumbled upstairs to his bedroom, then collapsed on the bed, fully clothed and face down and fell fast asleep. The other children followed him, and then looked at him fast asleep from the doorway.

Shelly turned to the others. 'It seems we are going to have an

The Tunnel

THIS IS THE BBC CALLING:

Today, Nazi Germany and the Soviet Union agree on a division of Poland after their invasion. This ends hostilities in Poland, and Poland is now under German control.

Warsaw has officially surrendered to the German forces.

Rishaan awoke to find himself clean, in his pyjamas and ready for a big breakfast. Matron had made sure he was not going to sleep face-down in a pool of aviation oil and grease.

Next to his bed was Buster Wordsworth, reading a newspaper.

'Buster!' said Rishaan, his voice a little hoarse.

'Finally, you are awake!' said Buster. 'How is my champion airman?'

'I feel fine, just stiff, like everything hurts. I feel as if I've run a hundred miles.'

'Well, Matron is on her way with some breakfast, hopefully some for me as well. You've been asleep for two days so you must be hungry.'

'Starved!' said Rishaan.

'Well, now we have something in common. I may be the only person to have crashed the same plane twice in the space of a few minutes, but you, my boy, took off in one plane and crashed in another!'

'How is going – are you an Ace yet?' asked Rishaan.

'Not yet!' said Buster. 'We had a great go at Jerry a week ago, though. We were patrolling off the Lincolnshire coast, from North Coates, when we intercepted a bunch of Heinkel floatplanes. They were out looking for ships to sink in the North Sea. Two Spitfires had softened them up for us, so they were flying low. So nine of us dived on them and gave them a run for their money. I was somewhat lucky. They are removing the linen coverings on our Hurricane wings and replacing them with metal. This means we can dive bomb without the fabric being ripped of the wings. However, they had not finished my plane yet and I was flying with one linen wing and one metal, so I couldn't dive bomb. I let my mates dive first and dust the Heinkels up, and then I came slowly behind and finished one off. Splash! Straight into the North Sea! We won't see them again for a while. We got four of the nine, without any losses on our side.'

Rishaan wanted to know more, then sat bolt upright. 'Two days! I need to get to London now!' said Rishaan, and he jumped out of bed. 'Take me to London now!' he pleaded to Buster, so Buster grabbed his leather jacket.

'I guess no breakfast for me then.' sighed Buster.

On the way out, Rishaan saw King Zog admiring the crashed plane in the driveway. 'Your Highness! What are you doing here?'

'Your father generously offered to allow a friend of the family, Charles, to stay here while I am in exile and lobbying for Albania. I heard about your exploits. I heard about your mother. I am so sorry. I'm sure your father will be back in England shortly.'

Just then, Buster arrived to pick up Rishaan in his Morgan sports car.

'Where are you going?' asks King Zog.

'London, to see Churchill!'

'Then I'm coming with you!' shouted the King. The three of them pressed into the two-seater, and headed off at breakneck speed. King Zog had told him he needed to talk to Churchill as well. 'I have been trying to get a meeting with that man for a month,' he complained above the roar of the sports car. 'I am Zog, the King of Albania,' he exclaimed, 'and I want my country back!'

Rishaan greeted his grandfather then rushed up to the attic to try the telephone, but there was no reply. King Zog was very curious about the telephone, but decided not to ask too many questions. The sergeant major's trophies fascinated Buster.

'This is King Zog,' said Rishaan, introducing the king to the sergeant major.

'The king?' said the sergeant major, and he wiped his thick glasses with his shirttail. He put them back on again and stared at King Zog.

'Yes,' said Rishaan.

'Blimey! The king in my humble living room.' The sergeant major stood to attention and saluted.

'Your Highness!' he exclaimed.

'Is there any other way to contact Churchill?' asked Rishaan, desperately.

The sergeant major scratched his beard and thought deeply. He looked at Rishaan. 'I have the feeling that I have told you too much already,' he said. 'I don't want you getting up to any more adventures; your father will have me court-martialled.'

'There is another way?' asked Rishaan again. He was not going to let go.

The sergeant major looked uncomfortable. He was not happy with what he was about to tell Rishaan but it looked like he had no choice. 'What I am about to tell you stays between you and the King,' he said, nodding at King Zog. Then he started to draw a map.

As they raced back to London, the king studied the map. 'This hardly seems likely,' the king said, smoking his cigarette in a long cigarette holder.

'My grandfather may seem a little strange now, but he was a great soldier and has worked alongside Churchill over many years,' said Rishaan.

'Well, it is well known, a desperate king has to take desperate measures,' he replied.

Buster dropped them off at Horse Guards Road. The map showed them that there was a tunnel from the Duck Island Cottage in St. James Park to the cabinet office. It was roughly drawn and it seemed unclear where exactly the tunnel ended.

'This was drawn by someone who thinks that I'm the king of England,' said King Zog. 'Just how accurate do you think it is?'

Duck Island Cottage seemed a bit derelict and run down, and there was nobody in the building. It seemed to once have been a residence but looked more like an abandoned office. The door was locked. Rishaan peered in through the dirty windows but could see very little. They tried the door several times.

'I am a King!' Zog exclaimed, then rushed the door, bursting it open and he ended up tumbling on the floor. The cottage seemed abandoned, the floors were dusty, the windows were dirty, and the whole cottage was unkempt. Some workers had used the table recently to have a lunch, but the rest was empty.

Rishaan looked at the map his grandfather had drawn. 'It says that there is a tunnel leading from the fireplace down and across Horse Guards Parade,' he said.

They both stared into the fireplace, but there was nothing there, except a fireplace.

Rishaan grabbed a piece of wood and pushed the burnt cinders to one side. The bottom of the fireplace seemed to be a plate of some sorts. Rishaan used the wood to make the edges more clear and soon found on one edge a grip that he could pull on. The plate opened to reveal a shaft leading down. The king looked over, and then dropped a small piece of rubbish into the shaft. It hit the ground quickly, showing it was not too deep.

They both looked at the shaft for a while, wondering what to do next.

'So your crazy grandfather says that Mr. Churchill is down there?' he asked.

'Yes,' said Rishaan.

They looked at the shaft again.

'Well, let's go and talk to Mr. Churchill,' said Rishaan, and he started to climb into the dark tunnel.

'I am Zog,' King Zog began, but changed his mind and followed Rishaan.

Once inside the tunnel, Rishaan's eyes soon adapted to the dark, with some light coming down from the shaft. The tunnel dead-ended to the left, but seemed to go on to the right, just as his grandfather's map said it would. There was a lamp and some candle stubs on the ground, so King Zog pulled out his cigarette lighter and lit one; they put as many of the rest in their pockets as they could. Rishaan put his hand on something soft and warm, and it squealed and scurried off.

'A rat!' Rishaan shouted.

'Be calm, they are more frightened of you than you are of them,' said the King, but he seemed just as put off by the thought of rats as Rishaan was.

The candle did not give off much light, but there was enough to see that some sides of the tunnel were wet and slimy. Rishaan was secretly glad he could not see more.

'It looks like the sergeant major could be right – this tunnel is going in the direction of the government buildings,' said Rishaan, trying to find something positive to say.

The sides of the tunnel were made of brick; one side seemed to be the foundations of the cottage. The floor was made of brick, slabs of stone, pebbles and some pressed dirt. The roof was made of wooden planks, with cobwebs hanging down from them. There were beams supporting the planks, but they seemed old and not well maintained. Rishaan wondered when the tunnel had been built and if anybody except his grandfather knew about it. If the tunnel collapsed would they be trapped forever here? There was not enough room to stand or crouch; they could only crawl.

Rishaan started to crawl, but King Zog stopped him.

'I am a king, and a king always leads!' he declared. With the lamp held up, giving minimal light, he pushed past Rishaan.

They crawled down the tunnel. It was too small to do anything else, and it was slow going. King Zog cursed constantly, but Rishaan just ignored him. He was glad he did not understand Albanian.

The stubbed candle soon burnt out, so King Zog replaced it with a new one.

'We have eight candle stubs; when we reach five we are either going back in the light, or carry on, and risk having to come back in the dark,' said King Zog.

They continued, and after a few minutes, the following candle stub burnt out.

'Three!' said King Zog, as if he was declaring a new law for Albania. The following stub lasted a little longer, but again, soon burnt out. 'Four!' declared the King.

The crawling was difficult and tiring, and soon they stopped to rest. They decided to preserve candles, so they just sat in the dark. Suddenly, a huge noise started to develop, and some dust started to fall from the tunnel ceiling. King Zog was too entranced to light up a candle. It soon passed by.

'It's okay, it's only the road above us. That must be a lorry,' said Rishaan.

They soon moved on, and after a few minutes the forth candle burnt out.

'Finished!' declared King Zog, like an umpire counting out a floored boxer.

They sat there again in the darkness. There was a squeal, and Rishaan felt a rat clamber past him.

'What shall we do?' asked Rishaan. He did not like this at all.

'We advance – the dark cannot hurt us!' said King Zog. Rishaan was getting scared, but he kept up with the King. They advanced through the following candles, but soon all eight were gone.

'What now?' asked Rishaan.

'We have come this far; we advance in the dark. I can feel my way; you will be safe behind me,' he said, but he did not sound enthusiastic. 'I am a king, and a king does this for his people!' he said, asserting bravery into his actions.

They crawled on until after a while he heard a bump, then the King Zog swore.

'What's wrong?' Rishaan asked.

'It's a dead end,' said the King, and they sat there in silence.

Rishaan felt around, and then the king lit his lighter to get a few seconds of weak light. 'Look,' he said, 'behind you!'

Behind Rishaan, against one wall, was a ladder leading up to a shaft.

'I will go first,' said the king, and he pressed past Rishaan. 'The things you have to do when you are king,' he muttered.

He twisted himself so he could get up into the shaft and started climbing. It was a long climb; both Rishaan and the king had felt that the tunnel had been leading them in a downward slope.

Dust fell as the king climbed, covering Rishaan, but Rishaan followed him anyway. He did not want to stay down in the dark tunnel alone with the rats.

'There's a metal grate at the top; it's blocked!' said the king, and he started to push, sending more dirt and dust down onto Rishaan.

Churchill sat alone in the cabinet room of 10 Downing Street. He had just had one of the gloomiest meetings ever since he had become First Lord of the Admiralty. They had discussed the amount of resources they had to send to replenish the army, and it was not encouraging. They needed to re-stock everything, and they needed to train hundreds of thousands of new soldiers. They needed new uniforms, new rifles, tanks and airplanes. All things they did not have the basic materials for and needed to import from America. However, Hitler's submarines, the dreaded U-boats, were sinking the cargo ships that were bringing the materials to Britain. He sat deep in thought. He knew the war against Hitler would be won with new technology and fought in the air, not with bayonets and in the trenches.

Churchill was so deep in thought he did not at first hear a grinding noise. It seemed to come from the fireplace behind him. A little dust plumed upward as the movement behind him seemed to continue. Churchill peered at the grate as it wiggled about. Suddenly, it popped open, and a moustached man covered in soot stuck his head up through the opening.

'I am Zog, King of Albania, and I want my country back!' he exclaimed.

'That's the first time I've ever seen Churchill speechless,' said the security guard, later, as Rishaan sat in a side room waiting for Churchill to finish talking to King Zog.

'What's happening?' asked Rishaan.

The security guard shrugged. 'Often drop in through the chimney?' he asked.

'Only when I'm with King Zog,' said Rishaan.

After what seemed like a long time, Rishaan was called into the cabinet room where Churchill was waiting for him. The king had left.

'You look a mess!' said Churchill.

Rishaan beamed – he bet he looked funny, his face covered in soot. Rishaan told Churchill everything about his trip to

Germany, about the Canary, the resistance workers, and the coded letter.

'What were the numbers?' asked Churchill.

Rishaan thought about it for a minute. He imagined walking into his house in London. He imagined 24 pairs of shoes by the door. He looked at the staircase; it had 31 steps going up. He walked into the kitchen, there were 45 sets of knives and forks in the drawers. There were 34 plates on the table, and 12 chairs around the table.

24. 31.45.34.12

'Are you sure?' asked Churchill.

'Perfectly,' said Rishaan.

'Excellent,' said Churchill.

'What does it mean?' asked Rishaan, not sure if he was allowed to ask.

'Nothing.'

'Nothing?'

'Nothing,' repeated Churchill.

'Why would you go to all that trouble, risk all those lives, just to get a message that means nothing?'

'Trust. Trust is everything, and I need to trust Admiral Canaris. So I sent a message through one of our spies to be given to Canaris, that he had to give to me. He did not know that I was the originator and already knew what the message was. If the message got lost or fell into the wrong hands, no harm done, as it meant nothing. If Canaris gave me the message, but thinking it might be important, he changed it in some way, then I would know that Canaris was not to be trusted. Also, if something happened to the message, then I would know that there were leaks in the organization.

However, everything went according to plan. I think Canaris is on our side. I hope so, but with spies, you can trust no one. You always must be careful.'

There was something else. Rishaan told Churchill about the radar detectors in the Zeppelin. He told him he had overheard that they were searching in the higher frequencies and not in the lower frequencies. Churchill was interested, and said he would certainly pass that information on to the scientists. 'If what you say is true, then the Germans have not discovered our radar capabilities, and that will be of great importance to us.' Churchill looked pleased. 'This is some good news in a day of bad news,' he said.

Churchill's personal assistant walked in. 'You have a visitor,' said the man.

'I will see him shortly.' said Churchill.

'It's for the boy, sir, not you,' said the man.

'Oh really?' said Churchill.

The assistant led Rishaan away. As they walked down the stairs, adorned with portraits of the previous prime ministers, their gazes seemed to follow Rishaan who looked for all the world like a sooty chimney sweep. He remembered the coal man he had seen at the beginning of the year, now near the end of the year, he was covered in soot. He was brought to the famous black front door of 10 Downing Street. A footman opened the door, and there, standing outside, was Rishaan's father.

His father put away his pipe and opened his arms, into which Rishaan flew.

'You're back!' shouted Rishaan. Rishaan felt overwhelmed with emotion. He felt tears welling up, but he fought them back. They hugged for a while and then they both just smiled.

'No more adventures for you my lad,' said his father. 'I can't risk losing you as well; your mother would never forgive me. Its back to Chelmsford for you till this mess blows over.'

Rishaan nodded. He was so glad to see his father again. Churchill came out and shook hands with Rishaan's father.

'You have an exceptional son,' said Churchill.

'Sometimes a little too exceptional,' said Rishaan's father, and smiled.

'Don't worry, Father, I promise to keep out of trouble. At least until the war is over, that is!'

To be continued

1940 – The Battle of Britain